A TOAST TO TROUBLE

A RIGHT ROYAL COZY INVESTIGATION MYSTERY

HELEN GOLDEN

DREW BRADLEY PRESS

ALSO BY HELEN GOLDEN

A Right Royal Cozy Investigation Series

A Toast To Trouble (Novella)

Tick, Tock, Mystery Clock (Novelette)

Spruced Up For Murder

For Richer, For Deader

Not Mushroom For Death

An Early Death (Prequel)

Deadly New Year (Novelette)

A Dead Herring

I Spy With My Little Die

A Cocktail to Die For

Dying To Bake

A Death of Fresh Air

I Kill Always Love You

Murder Most Wilde

This is a work of fiction. Names, characters, places, and incidents are the product of the author's imagination or used fictitiously. Any resemblance to actual persons, living or dead, events, or locales, is entirely coincidental.

ISBN (P) 978-1-915747-29-7

Edited by Marina Grout at Writing Evolution

Published by Drew Bradley Press

Cover design by Helen Drew-Bradley

First edition February 2025

NOTE FROM THE AUTHOR

I am a British author and this book has been written using British English. So if you are from somewhere other than the UK, you may find some words spelt differently to how you would spell them. In most cases this is British English, not a spelling mistake. We also have different punctuation rules in the UK.

However if you find any other errors, I would be grateful if you would please contact me helen@helengoldenauthor.co.uk and let me know so I can correct them. Thank you.

For your reference I have included a list of characters in the order they appear, and you can find this at the back of the book.

INTRODUCTION - NOVEMBER 2021

The author sat staring at her laptop screen, a look of horror creeping over her face as the reality of what she'd heard dawned on her.

"So to summarise, a reader magnet is an essential tool in building a relationship with your reader. Thank you for attending this webinar. If you'd like to ask questions, please do so by using the chat button now. I will spend the next fifteen minutes answering as many of them as I can."

The author selected the chat button and typed: *Just so I'm clear, having spent months writing a book that I haven't even released yet, you now want me to write another book, and give it away for free?*

She waited. She took a sip of her tea; yuck, it was cold. Rising, she put the kettle on.

"We have a question from Helen."

The author ran back to her laptop as the course leader read her question aloud.

"Well, Helen, I understand it may seem daunting so soon after finishing your first book, but yes, you need to write something that's available to potential readers who sign up to join your author group, and you need to give it to them for free. As I've explained, it is so you can introduce yourself to them, to let them see your style of writing and hopefully to make them want to read more from you." She smiled. "Thank you for your question, Helen, and good luck."

Letting out an enormous sigh, the author closed the lid of her laptop and stared out of the caravan window. A pink petal threw itself off the untidy rose bush at the side of the driveway. *I know how you feel*, she thought as she poured hot water over the tea bag in her cup. Standing, she opened a cupboard and took out a family-size bag of cheese and onion crisps. Grabbing a handful, she stuffed them into her mouth.

Her hands propping up her face, the author stared out of the window of her caravan and contemplated what she was going to write.

It had been her intention to work in the lovely new office recently built as an extension of the house. But she had to share the space with her husband, who, thanks to the recent pandemic, now worked from home. The author loved her husband dearly, but he was incapable of explaining to his colleagues how engineering stuff worked without shouting and waving his arms about. A lot.

That wasn't an environment conducive to someone who was trying to write a novel when they needed *total* quiet. So, not being the one who required a set up resembling mission control to do their job (*why do you need three screens, darling?*), the author had somewhat reluctantly volunteered to find another space to work.

Like in their caravan, which was currently parked on their drive.

On her right was a green metal shed, which housed her husband's motorbike. But if she leaned her head further around until it rested against the window, she could see the striking village church diagonally opposite their house. Parts of the church went back to the twelfth century. It was beautiful. Through the large front windows of the caravan she could see the trees and bushes that lined the driveway and spilled into her neighbour's garden. On the left was the front door of their house. Sometimes the author liked to jump out at unsuspecting delivery person and give them a bit of a fright.

As she continued gazing out of the window, the author spotted one of their cats. Louie, a beautiful red-striped male Bengal, was grooming himself in the sun on her opposite neighbour's lawn. Drumming her fingers on the table, the author looked ahead of her at the two sofas, where three dogs were sprawled.

Margot, a small female chorkie, was curled into a tight ball. So cute that everyone picked her up and kissed her, she was affectionately known as 'diseased dog' during the COVID-19 pandemic. Next to her was Alfie, a large long-haired male chihuahua, who was obsessed with food and recently had been described by the vet as 'too chunky'. Opposite them, snoring loudly, was Bourbon, a hefty male black pug belonging to her niece. Like a lovable bull in a china shop, when awake, he barged around the house, leaving a trail of destruction behind him.

I'm not procrastinating, she told herself. She was simply waiting for inspiration.

She wondered where Fluff was. The author's husband described the small grey long-haired female Bengal cat as 'an evil ball of fluff' because of her habit of peeing on his shoes. Not hearing the familiar cry of the little cat outside, a demand that the author had to stop working and let her in the front door of the house, the author cleared her throat and focused back on what she'd been told in the webinar.

The smiley lady on her screen had suggested writing a short story and using it to introduce some characters featured in her series. *Okay*, the author thought, *let's try that.*

A Toast To Trouble takes place a few years before *Spruced up for Murder*, the first in the *A Right Royal Cozy Investigation* series.

1

AFTERNOON. TWO DAYS BEFORE THE PARTY...

Lady Beatrice, the Countess of Rossex, hurried out of her apartment on the second floor of Francis Court and down the stately home's grand staircase, her footsteps ringing out as she crossed the Painted Hall and ducked through the door that led to the west wing.

She gnawed at her bottom lip. Her sister, Lady Sarah Rosdale, was under immense pressure. Her turning Francis Court into an exclusive events venue rested on Lucinda Hamilton's lavish thirtieth birthday party being perfect, but so far too many things were going wrong. Bea worried that her sister had seemed so... off earlier. So unlike her usual composed self.

I'll just check in on her so she knows I'm here if she needs me.

As she passed by the events office and carried on along the corridor, a wail erupted from behind the door of the catering kitchen, followed by a string of loud curses.

Bea's stomach sank. *That doesn't sound good*, she thought as she hesitated outside. She gingerly pushed open the swinging door.

Inside, a lofty man in chef's whites sat at a large table with his head in his hands, muttering expletives under his breath. He glanced up as Bea entered, his expression stormy.

"Hello. Is everything alright?" Bea asked him politely, even though it was clear from his frazzled appearance that it wasn't.

The man glowered at her. "No, it bloody well isn't alright!"

Well, you asked for that!

"Look in there." He jabbed a finger towards the open door of the walk-in refrigerator.

Cautiously, Bea approached and peered inside. Her eyes widened. On a portable metal table, an enormous five-tiered cake sat in ruins, smashed to pieces, frosting and chunks of cake splattered on the tabletop and across the floor.

Her pulse raced as she surveyed the damage to Lucinda's birthday party cake.

Her first thought was of her older sister. *Oh no, poor Sarah. Not another problem for her to deal with.*

Bea took a deep breath. *I need to tell her!*

She fumbled for her phone and snapped a few quick photos before texting them to Sarah:

Bea: *I'm sorry. I know you're having a bad day, but you need to come to the kitchen ASAP.*

She pressed send, then her eyes roamed around the fridge. She quickly spotted a heavy-duty saucepan on the shelf, covered in cake and icing. *Well, that would be the weapon of destruction.* She took a photo, then returned to the kitchen.

"What happened?" she asked the chef, her voice calm but firm.

The man ran a hand through his hair, clearly flustered. "I don't know. I found it like this. It was fine when I left last night."

Bea's lips tightened. "And you are…?"

"Nathan Harper, head chef for Posh and Fabulous, the events company. Everyone calls me Nat," he replied, his earlier brusqueness fading into something closer to embarrassment. "I'm sorry about the language. It's just that the cake took me days to make and ice. What am I supposed to do now?" He seemed genuinely distraught.

Who did this? It had clearly been no accident, but Bea had no idea what should be done next. "Lady Sarah is on her way. She'll know what to do." *I hope!*

As if on cue, Sarah burst through the kitchen doors, looking harried. Bea pointed to the walk-in room. Without a word Sarah strode over and craned her head around the door. Letting out a deep sigh, she turned to them. "Do we know what happened?"

"It was intact when I left it here yesterday afternoon, my lady. I was going to decorate it today…" He trailed off with a shrug.

"Okay. Well, please carry on with your other preparations, and leave the rest to me."

The chef gave a nod, and rose as, with a gentle tug on Bea's elbow, Sarah led her out into the hall. Bea rounded on her the moment the door swung shut.

"Sarah, I think this was deliberate. Did you see the saucepan? First the list of guests, then the centrepiece, now the cake. It looks like someone is trying to sabotage this party."

Sarah threw up her hands. "I don't know what's going on,

Bea! But I can't think about that now. I've got to speak to Evie or Jas from Posh and Fabulous to sort out another cake," she said, concern etched into her face.

"Is there anything I can do to help?"

"Yes. Find out who's doing this to me, Bea," she said, her voice barely above a whisper, then she turned and hurried away.

What? Bea's heart dropped to her toes. *Is she serious? I'm not the police!* She had no idea how to investigate a crime. She chewed her lower lip. The urge to retreat to her rooms, to hide from this mess was strong. But as she stood here, she knew she couldn't sit back and watch her sister struggle. *Right!* She stood up tall. *Where do I begin?*

2

FIVE DAYS EARLIER

T*he Society Page* online article:

<u>Heiress Lucinda Hamilton Prepares to Turn 30</u>

Lucinda Hamilton (29), only daughter of Sir Leo Hamilton (59), owner of the Scottish based shipping line SCH, and his wife, Dame Katherine Hamilton (56), the opera singer, was spotted in Harrods yesterday, having the final fitting for the dress she will wear to her lavish 30th birthday bash in five days time.

Lucinda recently broke off her engagement to footballer Danny Roe (32) after photos appeared online of him getting up close and personal with his sports agent at a Manchester nightclub while Lucinda was away in the Maldives on a modelling assignment. Friends of the model and heiress say she is ready to party and forget all about Danny despite his very public attempts over recent days to win her back.

Lucinda's exclusive birthday party, the guest list of which is a who's who of high society, is taking place at Francis Court in Fenshire, home of Charles Astley (59), the Duke of Arnwall, and his wife, Her Royal Highness Princess Helen (58), the sister of King James. Their eldest daughter, Lady Sarah Rosdale (35), who lives on the estate with her family and manages the house, is organising the prestigious event taking place in the Red Ballroom, one of the country house's state-rooms, along with local party planners, Posh and Fabulous.

Also living on the Francis Court estate with her son, Samuel Wiltshire (10), is Lady Beatrice (32), the Countess of Rossex, whose husband, James Wilshire, died in a late-night car crash along with a female passenger eleven years ago. It is, however, unlikely Lady Beatrice will be attending the party as apart from a handful of official royal family events and the occasional charity fundraiser, she has kept herself out of the public eye since her husband's death.

3

THREE DAYS BEFORE THE PARTY

Perry Juke's skin prickled with goosebumps as he strode into the opulent Red Ballroom at Francis Court, his polished boots clicking against the marble floor. *Just three days until showtime!* He gazed at the chandeliers above him as they sparkled in the afternoon sun, butterflies in his stomach. This was his chance to shine, to prove his promotion from head tour guide to Lady Sarah Rosdale's executive assistant was well-deserved.

Thinking of his boss… She appeared at his side as if by magic, dressed in a fitted blue shift dress, clipboard in hand. "All set?" she asked, raising a perfectly shaped eyebrow up at him.

He nodded. "Always. Let's get this party started." He flashed Sarah a grin. She rolled her eyes, but he caught a hint of a smile tugging at the corners of her mouth.

He straightened his jacket, put on his most charming smile, and he and Sarah made their way to the middle of the room where two women stood deep in conversation. The curvy woman with long straight blonde hair he knew already. Jasmin Curson ran local event planners, Posh and Fabulous, and was, indeed, both of those things. She was dressed in a white cashmere jumper and beautifully tailored taupe-coloured trousers. Her plummy voice echoed around the vast empty ballroom. Next to her stood a taller woman with a sleek brown bob, wearing a black suit with a cream blouse and flat shoes.

"Ladies," Sarah greeted them with a curt smile. "How are we?"

"Lady Sarah," Jas responded. "Have you met Evie Hayes yet? She's one of my event planners, and she's helping me oversee the setup here. She'll also be managing the clear up afterwards."

Evie gave an awkward sort of bow as she took Sarah's hand. "I'm available twenty-four seven, my lady. Anything you need."

Sarah smiled. "Welcome to the team, Evie. This is Perry Juke. He's my right-hand man and your first point of call if you have any issues."

Evie smiled shyly as she looked up and met Perry's gaze. Perry returned her smile briefly before she looked away. *She seems calm, if a little guarded. Hopefully, she'll be less stuck-up than Jas.* Perry wasn't a huge fan of the manager of Posh and Fabulous, finding her cool and aloof. She also didn't like to get her hands dirty, preferring to leave the details to her team of party planners. But there was no denying she was good at being the face of the company, and come the evening of the event, she would schmooze the guests like nobody's business, making them feel special.

"So shall we start with the guest list?" Sarah asked, bringing the clipboard up to her chest. "Any updates?"

"Yes, there are a few last-minutes changes," Jas said, referring to her tablet.

Perry stifled a sigh as he looked at it with envy. He'd been trying to persuade Sarah to ditch her old clipboard and put everything on a tablet for years. Even in his previous job as head guide, rather than email him, she'd handed him printed lists of things with written notes on them that she'd needed him to know in advance of opening up the state rooms. He'd pointed out to her on many occasions that lists went missing or got left lying around and that without a record somewhere, they couldn't be replicated. She, in turn, had pointed out that she needed to write things down as soon as she thought of them. He'd tried to explain that the tablet came with a pen she could use in the same way, but her eyes had glazed over, and after muttering, "But I *like* paper," she'd dismissed his suggestion and had continued to carry around her trusty clip-board, writing notes on the original guest list. She'd even refused giving it to him so he could update the computer file in the office.

I'll tackle her again now I'm in this job. I'll bring her kicking and screaming into the twenty-first century if I have to, he vowed.

"Of course," Sarah replied, flipping over the top piece of paper attached to her clipboard. Her hand froze mid-air. "Oh, my goodness. It's not here."

Perry's stomach dropped. The list of attendees was sacred, the key to the entire event, and that was their only up-to-date copy. Sarah's composure faltered for a split second before he jumped in. "I'm sure I saw it in the office," he lied. "Why don't I make a note of the changes now, and I'll get it for you later?" He might be frustrated with Sarah's out-of-date admin methods, but he wouldn't let her look like anything but a total professional in front of Jas and Evie.

Sarah's relief was palpable. "Thank you, Perry. Yes, that would be helpful."

As Jasmine began detailing the changes, Perry reached

into his pocket to take out his phone, but Evie tore a page from her planner and whispered, "Here. You can use this." She handed him the paper and a pen with the Posh and Fabulous logo emblazoned in gold on the side .

Really? Another paper user? He suppressed a huff. *Is it just me who wants to be more efficient?* But, not wanting to appear rude, he accepted with a grateful nod. "Thanks," he murmured, making notes as Jas continued to rattle off the changes.

"And last," Jasmine said, tossing her blonde mane, "the Worthingtons are now a party of three instead of four. Apparently, their eldest has come down with a nasty bout of flu."

Perry nodded, jotting down the final note. "Got it. I'll make sure everything's updated immediately."

Sarah cleared her throat. "Jas, Evie, I cannot stress enough how crucial this event is. Lucinda Hamilton's not any ordinary client. She's…"

A dragon in Gucci? That just about summed up their diva-ish party girl as far as Perry was concerned. He moved to whisper something along those lines to Evie to warn her when he caught the look on her face. He was sure he'd seen her wince when Lucinda's name had been mentioned, but now she looked as if there was a nasty smell right under her nose. *Maybe she's already had dealings with the spoilt heiress?*

"…very, er, particular," Sarah continued tactfully. "This 'modern-day fairytale' theme needs to meet her expectations."

"Don't worry," Jas reassured her. "I have it all under control. Picture this." She pivoted and opened her arms wide. "A sea of twinkling fairy lights, an enormous hanging floral arrangement dripping with crystals, an enchanted forest backdrop, chandeliers draped with gossamer, and tables adorned with chrome and glass centrepieces filled with bioluminescent flowers. It will be Cinderella on steroids."

Perry stifled a laugh. *It sounds awful to me, but Lucinda will love it!*

Perry strode into the office and made a beeline for Sarah's desk. He rifled through the neat stack of papers and folders on top. No guest list.

"Rats!" he muttered under his breath. *What's she done with it?* Sarah had insisted that the last time she'd seen it, it had been attached to her clipboard as always. Perry hadn't been able to stop himself from saying in a low voice, "This wouldn't have happened if we had it on a tablet," before he'd left her to show Evie around while he headed back to her office to look for the elusive document.

He checked the drawers, the filing cabinet, even under the potted fern in the corner. Nothing. He sank into Sarah's plush leather chair, running a hand through his artfully-waxed spiky blond hair. She must have taken it home with her. *She probably got it mixed up with Robbie's or Lottie's school paperwork.* Sarah worked hard at her job. Her husband, John, got their two children out of bed, dressed, and fed each morning before he took their daughter to school, and her sister accompanied their son along with her own to a different school, so Sarah could get in early. Sarah in return, was a stickler when it came to being home not long after her children got back from school each day, often starting work again after they'd settled for the evening.

Fishing his phone out of his pocket, he fired off a quick text.

. . .

Perry: *Hey boss. I can't find the list in your office. Is it possible you took it home last night and left it there? Do you want me to go and pick it up?*

He hit send, then leaned against the desk. Sarah was usually particular about these things. He hoped it was at her house… He sprung upright as his phone pinged with a message.

Sarah: *I don't remember taking it home, but I'll have a look later. Thanks.*

Perry shrugged, pushing the niggling worry to the back of his mind. He'd plenty of other things to get on with.

Later that evening, Perry lounged on the plush sofa in Rose Cottage, his eye half on the reality TV show on in the corner of the room and half on his boyfriend, Simon Lattimore, sitting in the armchair adjacent to him, engrossed in his laptop screen, his brow furrowed in concentration.

An ex-CID Fenshire detective, Simon had become a best-selling crime writer since he'd left the police force four years ago and was currently working on his fifth DI Bill Pike novel. Perry smiled smugly. He was so proud of Simon. He fought the urge to tell him now, this minute, knowing better than to disturb him when he was editing his manuscript.

"You know," Simon suddenly said without moving his head. "If your face freezes like that, I'm not sure I can be seen in public with you ever again."

He looked up, caught Perry's eye, and winked. Perry's smile now turned into a grin. "You'd miss my devastatingly handsome mug too much."

Simon dipped his head. "Yeah, maybe."

Before Perry could reply, his phone pinged. He glanced at the screen.

Sarah: *List still MIA. Starting to worry. What could have happened to it?*

Perry sighed. "Sarah still can't find the missing guest list."

Simon raised an eyebrow. "The unflappable Lady Sarah misplacing something? Alert the media."

"I'm serious, love. That list is like her baby. She normally guards it with her life."

"Well, she has been distracted by this party. I'm sure it'll turn up."

Perry shrugged. "Yeah, you're probably right. In the meantime, I have the email updates that Jas sent as confirmation of the changes and my notes from this afternoon. I think I can recreate it," he said, tapping out a reply along those lines to Sarah.

But as he hit send, a nagging feeling settled in the pit of his stomach. Sarah was the most meticulous person he knew. For her to lose something so important was unheard of, so where on earth was it?

4

MORNING. TWO DAYS BEFORE THE PARTY…

The delicate *clink* of china echoed through the Breakfast Room at Francis Court as Sarah set down her mid-morning coffee with a sigh. Across the table, Bea quirked an eyebrow, sensing the tension radiating from her sister's perfectly poised form. *What's going on with her?*

"So this missing list," Bea said, leaning back in her chair and crossing her legs, careful not to knock Daisy, her West Highland terrier, who snoozed contentedly under the table. "You seem upset about it."

Sarah sighed, taking a sip of her coffee. "It's just... It's such a massive event, Bea. Every detail matters. And now with the guest list vanishing into thin air…" She shook her head, frustration etching lines around her mouth.

"But you have a copy, surely?" Bea smiled reassuringly. "A backup."

Sarah grimaced, biting her bottom lip. "Sort of. You know how I like to write my notes on things. Well…"

Bea let out an exasperated breath. "Don't tell me you were writing on the original, and you've not transferred it to your computer." Her sister looked sheepish as she took another sip of coffee. "Really, Sarah, why don't you get a tablet that you can carry around and update as you go along, instead of that old—"

"Alright!" Sarah scowled as she held up her hand. "You're as bad as everyone else. I get it, and I'll think about it when this party's over. In the meantime, it's not helping me."

"Sorry," Bea said. "Can you get a copy from the party planners? Or recreate it perhaps?"

"Yes, of course. My assistant's already on it, reconstructing the list from emails and notes." Sarah took a sip of her coffee.

Bea tilted her head, curious. "So then what's really bothering you, sis?"

Sarah hesitated, her fingers tightening around the delicate handle of her cup. "I... I don't want to let Ma down," she admitted quietly. "You know how much these events mean to her. She wants to put this place on the map as the go-to destination for society events. I don't know if it's going to work…" She trailed off as she put her cup back on its saucer. "Lucinda is driving me up the wall, Bea." Sarah groaned. "Changes, demands… It never ends."

"Ah, yes, the infamous Lucinda," Bea scoffed. "Didn't cousin Sophie say she was a total bi—"

"Bea!" Sarah hissed, glancing around nervously.

Bea rolled her eyes. "Fine. A total witch. With a capital B. Sophie was at school with her, remember? Lucinda was a diva then, and clearly, nothing has changed."

Sarah slumped, her perfect posture cracking. "I need this event to be flawless."

Bea licked her lips as she studied her sister for a moment.

Was there anything she could do? Sarah didn't normally need her help, but it would be right to offer, wouldn't it? She uncrossed her legs and leaned forward. "Is there anything I can do to help?"

Sarah's head snapped up, genuine surprise etched on her features. "You? But you never show any interest in the estate's affairs."

Bea bristled. *That's hardly fair!* "Because you always seemed to have everything so utterly under control. I didn't think you needed me sticking my nose in." She fixed Sarah with a stare as she crossed her arms.

Sarah's expression softened. "Oh, Bea. I'm sorry. I didn't realise…" She trailed off, faintly blushing.

Bea reached across the table, covering her sister's hand with her own. "Don't worry." Bea waved her off, not wanting Sarah to feel bad about it. "Now are you going to let me help or not?"

Relief washed over Sarah's features. "Actually," she said slowly, "I could use your feedback on a few things. Will you come with me to the Red Ballroom, and I'll fill you in on the plans?"

Bea nodded, smiling, and gave Sarah's hand a quick squeeze before standing. Daisy lifted herself off the floor and did a long downward dog stretch before following them out.

Daisy trotted beside the two sisters as they swept into the Red Ballroom of Francis Court, a flurry of activity assaulting their senses. Staff bustled about, their arms laden with flowers and ribbons. The clatter of a ladder echoed as someone adjusted a string of twinkling lights. In the corner, they were setting up a sleek social media area, complete with a custom photo backdrop.

"Well, it's certainly fairytale-ish," Bea said as someone passed her, carrying a handful of extravagant floral centre-pieces. Lucinda's brief of 'modern-day fairytale' for her lavish thirtieth birthday party had been a challenging one.

Sarah lips tightened. "It's not quite there yet, but—"

"It'll be stunning," Bea told her, placing her hand on her sister's arm.

Sarah beamed, her perfectly made-up face glowing with pride. "Thanks, Bea. Do you think Lucinda will approve?"

"Well, if she doesn't love it, then you would never have been able to please her, whatever you did."

"Thanks for offering to come and take a look. Getting your thoughts will be a tremendous help, you know, sis," Sarah said, patting Bea's hand.

Aw, that's nice. Bea smiled. "Isn't that what sisters are for?"

Sarah grinned. "Well, then the next time Ma asks me to organise a birthday party for one of her friend's daughters, remind me to say no!"

Bea grinned back, but she knew Sarah was only half-kidding. The reputation of Francis Court as an exclusive events venue rested on Lucinda's party being perfect.

"So come on then. Tell me all about what's going where," Bea said, removing her hand. "Are you—"

Crack! Bea instinctively bent down and snatched her little white dog up off the floor as a massive floral decorative installation, suspended from the ceiling, gave way and hurtled towards the ground, narrowly missing a woman, who jumped out of the way just in time, her eyes wide with shock.

For a second, the room fell silent, save for the tinkling of shattered crystal, then Sarah cried, "Oh my goodness," her hand flying to her mouth. She rushed over to the shaken woman and grasped her trembling hands. "Are you alright?"

The woman nodded mutely, her eyes brimming with tears. Sarah signalled to a member of her team. "Please take her to the kitchen. Get her a strong, sweet tea and make sure she's okay."

As the woman was led away, Sarah turned to Bea, her face stripped of colour. "That could've killed her," she whispered, her voice strained.

Bea surveyed the wreckage, her mind racing. How did that happen? These things were checked and doubled-checked by the maintenance team, weren't they? She looked up at the ceiling, frowning.

Sarah, a wrinkle cutting across her forehead, said, "I don't know what happened, but this is a disaster. We need... I need…" Her eyes darted frantically around the room, then she took in a deep breath. "I need to find Perry."

Bea frowned. Which one is he again? There were so many people who worked here. Not having an active role on the estate, Bea didn't know them like Sarah did. "Is he one of the maintenance—"

Sarah whirled on her sister, her exasperation clear. "Perry Juke! My executive assistant, Bea. You've seen him with me a dozen times at least!"

"Oh!" Recognition dawned on Bea. "The former head guide? Looks like he stepped off a fashion show runway?"

"Yes, that's him." Sarah sighed. "And he's doing a great job. He'll know how to fix this. Look, Bea, I hate to cut this short, but can I give you the tour later?"

Bea nodded, giving her sister a quick hug. She didn't want to get in the way. "Of course. You go do what you need to do. I'll take Daisy for a run on the beach. Call me if you need anything, okay?"

As Bea left the ballroom, the little terrier still in her arms, she glanced back at her sister. Sarah was already deep in conversation with a member of staff, her posture tense. Bea's chest felt heavy. *Poor Sarah.* She didn't think she'd ever seen her sister so discombobulated. *No wonder. As she'd said, that poor woman could've been killed...*

5

MEANWHILE…

In his office, Perry saved the document, his fingers flying over the keyboard with practiced efficiency. With a final decisive click, he hit print. The machine gave a satisfying *whir* and spewed out the reconstructed guest list. Scooping up the warm pages, he slid them into a folder, then paused, considering. *Better safe than sorry.* He sent the file to the printer once more. *A backup copy can't hurt.*

The missing list still hadn't turned up even though he'd done another thorough search of Sarah's office this morning before he'd recreated it. *Has someone taken it?* He couldn't for the life of him think why someone would want it. There were no contact details on it or anything like that. It was just a list of names and their assigned table numbers. *It wouldn't be any use to anyone, would it?*

Buzz! Sarah's name flashed up on the screen. He swiped to read the message.

Sarah: *Problem in the RB. Come quickly!*

As he hurried towards the ballroom, his mind raced. *What now?* With only two days to go until the birthday celebrations, they didn't need problems. Hopefully, it was nothing too serious.

The Red Ballroom was a hive of frenzied activity when he arrived. Flower arrangements littered every surface, silver and white balloons bobbed gently in one corner, and—

"Oh my giddy aunt," Perry breathed as he came to an abrupt stop inside the door. The enormous focal decoration, an intricate web of flowers, crystals, and fairy lights, lay in a tangled heap on the marble floor. Shards of glass glittered everywhere. A cluster of shocked staff huddled nearby.

"Thank goodness you're here!" Sarah materialised at his elbow, her face pinched and pale. "The bolts came loose somehow."

Loose? How's that possible? Hadn't he watched Greg Morton from the maintenance team secure the installation only yesterday?

"Poor Sally nearly got brained by the thing. It was a good thing she looked up just at that moment and dodged out of the way," Sarah continued.

Perry's heart skipped a beat. "Is she okay?"

"She's shaken up but fine. I sent her off for some sweet tea." Sarah shook her head. "I can't believe this. Less than forty-eight hours to go and now... What's happening, Perry?" She leaned towards him and whispered, "First the list disappearing and now this. Is someone doing it on purpose to cause trouble?"

Perry's scalp tingled. That was what he'd been thinking. "I honestly don't know," he said. "But at the moment, we need to concentrate on getting this sorted out, agreed?"

She nodded. “I’ll talk to the supplier and see if we can get a replacement. Can you oversee the clear up?”

Perry nodded and squeezed her arm reassuringly. “Absolutely. You focus on the bigger picture, Sarah. Leave the details to me.”

She flashed him a grateful smile before hurrying off, the heels of her designer pumps clicking on the tiles.

Perry surveyed the wreckage. *I need to talk to Greg...*

Perry found the older man in the maintenance shed, hunched over a workbench. He looked up as Perry entered, his blue eyes sharp beneath bushy brows.

“Have you got a minute, Greg?” Perry asked as he hesitated in the doorway. He surveyed the dirty floor, his nose wrinkling. *I’ll just stay here.*

“I’m a bit busy, mate,” Greg replied dismissively as he went back to what he was doing.

Rude! Perry squared his shoulders. “The large centrepiece in the Red Ballroom. The one you put up yesterday. It came crashing down.”

Greg’s shoulders stiffened. “Did it now?”

“Yes.” Perry leaned against the doorway and crossed his arms. “And it nearly took someone out.”

Greg looked up from his bench, his eyes wide. “Are they okay?”

Perry tilted his head to one side. “She’s shaken, as you can imagine, but she’ll be fine, thank goodness. Lady Sarah is very upset. It was supposed to be the focal point of the room.”

A flicker of something—*triumph?*—crossed Greg’s weathered face. It vanished as quickly as it appeared, replaced by a scowl. "Well, ain't that a shame? I guess her ladyship will have to make do without it now."

Perry's eyes narrowed. Greg's reaction was off. Hostile even. The staff universally adored Sarah, appreciating her calm manner and fair leadership. *So why does Greg seem almost pleased by this setback?* "Do you know how the bolts could've come loose?"

"You accusin' me of somethin'?" Greg straightened, his jaw tight.

I wasn't... But now?

"Those bolts were tight!" Greg snapped, his shoulders tensing. "I doubled-checked 'em meself!"

Perry raised an eyebrow at the defensive tone. "I'm sure you did. But you have to agree it's odd given how securely they were fastened."

Greg's eyes darted away. "Yeah, well, sometimes things happen, don't they?"

Secured bolts loosen themselves, do they?

"Right," Greg grunted. "Well, if that's all..." He turned back to his workbench, muttering under his breath.

Perry suppressed a sigh as he turned to return to the house, a nagging sense of unease settling in his stomach.

Perry surveyed the Red Ballroom. Shards of crystal glittered across the polished floor like small diamonds. What's that? He crouched, plucking a bolt from the debris. Intact. *So it didn't shear off then?* If Greg was to be believed, then someone must have unscrewed it. Deliberately...

"Mr Juke?"

Perry spun around to see Sally Wells, one of the cleaners,

her hunched posture making her seem smaller than her already petite frame.

"Mrs Crammond sent me to help clean up," she murmured.

Perry stared at the woman who had almost been hit by the enormous centrepiece only a few hours earlier. *Why is she still here? Surely, she should have been sent home after such a shock?* "Are you sure you should be here, Sally? You've had a huge shock. I think—"

"I'm alright," she said, cutting him off. "Mrs Crammond wanted me to go home, but I need to keep busy, you know? It calms my nerves."

Cleaning? Really? I prefer a nice glass of red...

"Are you sure?" he asked gently. It really was sweet of her to come and clear up the mess that had nearly killed her.

"Totally." Sally lifted her chin. "Please just tell me what you want me to do, Mr Juke."

"Well, if you insist." Perry gestured dramatically at the chaos. "Please salvage any unbroken crystal. Everything else can be thrown away."

Sally nodded. Something flickered in her tired eyes as she surveyed the destruction. *Was that a glimmer of... satisfaction?* Perry frowned. *Does she actually enjoy cleaning this much?*

"Such a shame," she said, although her words lacked feeling. "I hope it won't ruin things."

Perry's eyebrows shot up. Since when did the cleaning staff care about society events?

"Lady Sarah's sourcing a replacement," he replied, watching her closely. "But it was rather the main focus of the room."

Sally's lips twitched. She bent to sift through the wreckage, muttering, "Mmm. Some people get what they deserve."

Perry blinked. *Did she say what I think she did*? Unease prickled Perry's neck. Surely, the timid maid wasn't implying.... *No, that's silly.*

Beep! Shaking off the ridiculous thought, he pulled his phone from his pocket.

Sarah: *This day just keeps getting better! Now we have a cake crisis. Can you come to the office ASAP?*

Perry's heart sank as he hurried out of the ballroom. They seemed to be lurching from one disaster to another...

6

TEN MINUTES LATER...

Perry walked into Sarah's office, his normally impeccable hair slightly mussed from his brisk walk from the main house to the Old Stable Block where their offices were housed. Lady Sarah looked up from her desk, her elegant features creased with worry.

He dropped into a chair on the other side of her desk. "What's up?"

"The cake's ruined," she said grimly.

"What? Do you mean it's not come out okay?" he asked, frowning.

"No. I mean, it was okay. Then someone battered it in with a saucepan, and now it's ruined."

On no! Perry groaned. "Where? When?"

"It was delivered here yesterday by Nathan Harper, the head chef from P&F, and stored in the walk-in refrigerator in the catering kitchen. It was already assembled and iced. All there was left to do was decorate it. But when he arrived about an hour ago, it had been destroyed."

Perry frowned. "The catering kitchen isn't locked, is it?"

Sarah shook her head.

So anyone could have gone in and attacked it.

"I've spoken to Jas. She's trying to get another one made in time, but it's going to be a close-run thing." She pursed her red lips. "My sister thinks the three incidents are connected, and someone is trying to sabotage the event."

Perry's chest tightened. *What has Sarah's younger sister got to do with this?* From what he'd seen, she'd paid no attention to what went on inside Francis Court. Whenever he'd seen her, she'd been floating around the place with her little dog, ignoring everyone around her with a hint of disdain.

"Lady Beatrice?" Perry scoffed. "Since when does she deign to get involved in anything we do here?"

Sarah shot him a look. "She's trying to help, Perry. And I think she might be right."

Much as he hated to admit it, Sarah's stuck-up sister had a point. The missing guest list, the fallen decoration, and now the cake catastrophe. It was all too much to be coincidence.

"But who would want to ruin the party? And why?" he mused aloud, rubbing his chin.

Sarah sighed, her usually unflappable demeanour cracking. "I don't know."

Determination surged through Perry's veins. This party was so important to Sarah and the future of Francis Court as an events venue; he'd not let some mystery saboteur destroy it. He'd talk to Simon when he got home and see if his partner's detective skills could help him figure out who was doing this.

"Leave it to me," he declared, squaring his shoulders. "I'll find out who's behind this, Sarah, and put an end to their little game."

Sarah raised a sceptical eyebrow. "I appreciate the sentiment, Perry, but how exactly do you plan to do that?"

A slow grin spread across Perry's face. "By being my

usual charming, observant self, of course. I know everyone here, remember, and no one can resist spilling their secrets to me."

A smile tickled at the corners of Sarah's mouth. "Well, I can't deny you usually know all the gossip."

"Exactly," he said with a wink, then he spun on his heel and strode out of the office, his mind already considering who to talk to first.

7

EARLY EVENING. TWO DAYS BEFORE THE PARTY…

Perry burst through the front door, the tantalising aroma of garlic and herbs welcoming him into Rose Cottage like a particularly attentive Maître d. One of the many advantages of having moved in with Simon three months ago was that he was an exceptional cook. And Perry loved food. He'd even told Simon he should enter the celebrity version of the TV cooking competition, *Elitechef*, but his other half had dismissed the idea, saying that he was a crime writer, not a chef, and he only cooked for fun.

Perry's stomach rumbled in anticipation as he hung up his coat. *Oh my goodness, that smells good.* As he walked into the cottage's open plan kitchen cum diner, Simon stood at the stove, stirring a simmering pot. He glanced over his shoulder with a smile. "Hey. Dinner's almost ready."

Perry bounded over and planted a quick kiss on Simon's stubbly cheek. So much had happened today—the centrepiece crashing down, the cake fiasco, his vow to get to the bottom of it all. The words danced on the tip of his tongue, desperate to spill out.

But first he needed to be a good partner. Perry leaned

against the counter and crossed his arms. "How was your day, love?"

Simon's eyes lit up. "Great, actually. I'm nearly done with the first act of the new book. The words were really flowing today."

Perry forced himself to focus, nodding along as Simon relayed a few more details about his day of writing. Inside, anticipation bubbled in his throat. *C'mon, c'mon...*

Just as Simon finished and Perry opened his mouth, a shrill *beep* pierced the air. The oven timer.

"That's the focaccia." Simon grabbed the oven gloves. "I don't know about you, but I'm hungry."

Perry huffed out a breath. His news would have to wait a few more minutes. The suspense was killing him. But the delectable scent wafting from the oven helped soften the blow. His impatience could hold out a little longer...

Fifteen minutes later, settled at the huge wooden table in the dining area, a half empty dish of pasta carbonara between them, Simon cocked an eyebrow at Perry. "Alright, out with it. I can see you practically vibrating out of your skin."

Perry paused with a forkful of creamy noodles halfway to his mouth. He lowered it back to his plate with a soft *clink*. "Well, since you asked…" He launched into a dramatic replay of the falling centrepiece and the narrow miss of Sally. He paused for effect, then continued, "And then there's the cake. Destroyed. Completely ruined. Done in with a heavy-duty saucepan."

Simon's brow had furrowed deeper with each additional detail. He let out a low whistle. "That's far more serious than a missing guest list."

"Exactly!" Perry stabbed his fork in the air. "Sally nearly got flattened by flowers. And guess what?" He leaned forward, his eyes glinting. "I'm going to find out who's behind it all."

Simon blinked. "You are?"

Perry deflated slightly. "You don't think I can do it?"

"No, no, I didn't mean..." Simon back-pedalled. "It's... Well, it seems like a big undertaking when you're so busy helping to organise this event..."

Perry crossed his arms. "Need I remind you, we solved a crime together before? You even said I had good instincts."

A smile tugged at a corner of Simon's mouth. "You're right. I did say that." He reached across the table and gave Perry's hand a squeeze. "Okay, Hercule Poirot. What's your first move?"

Perry's stomach sank as he chewed his lip. "Er... I'm not entirely sure." He smiled at Simon. "But that's where you come in, love." He turned his hand over to interlace their fingers. "You're the ex-detective. Will you give me some pointers on how to approach this?"

Simon dropped Perry's hand, then picked up his wine-glass and took a sip, considering. "Alright," he said finally. "But, Perry, this isn't a game. You need to be methodical and look at the evidence."

"Okay," Perry said, sitting up straight.

"Who, why, and how. That's what you need to focus on. Start with suspects—who had access and the ability to pull this off?"

Perry's mind whirled with possibilities, but, "I... I'm not sure," he admitted.

"Well, then, that's your first step," Simon said, reaching for more focaccia. "Identify potential suspects. Remember, access and ability first."

Perry jumped up, a wide grin on his face. "I'll make a

list!" He hurried over to the sideboard and returned with his tablet.

Simon smiled encouragingly as Perry sat back down in front of him. "Once you've got your suspects, then you can start sussing out motives."

"Motives. Right." Perry jabbed his finger on the screen and pulled up the notes app. "So I need to figure out who was on-site the past couple of days when things went pear-shaped. Like the catering staff, event crew, cleaning services, et cetera..."

Simon nodded approvingly. "See if you can get your hands on employee schedules, sign-in logs, that sort of thing."

Perry's eyes lit up with an idea. "Hey, you know who might have some good intel? Claire from HR."

"Good plan. Claire knows everyone and everything. She might help you with the motive too. Someone with a grudge who wants to cause trouble."

Perry picked up his phone.

Perry: *Feels like ages since I last saw you. Breakfast tomorrow in the Breakfast Room? 7:30 am?*

A reply pinged back seconds later.

Claire: *I never say no to breakfast. See you there.*

Perry felt a surge of excitement rush through him. *You can do this, Perry! And think how impressed Sarah will be when you reveal who the culprit is.* He returned to his tablet and began typing a list of names.

8

LATE EVENING. TWO DAYS BEFORE THE PARTY...

Bea idly stirred her chamomile tea, staring out at the clear night sky through the sitting room window. Daisy snoozed softly beside her on the sofa, a warm furry presence. The clock ticked steadily on the mantle. It was late, and Sam was tucked up in bed.

She sipped her tea, savouring its soothing floral warmth. She twisted a strand of red hair around her finger. The recent party incidents still nagged at her mind, but the motivation to investigate had waned. *This isn't my area of expertise.* Where on earth would she even begin? *Perhaps it's best if I don't get involved. I'll probably just get in the way...*

Her phone buzzed. She looked down at the bright screen.

Sarah: *Sorry I didn't get to see you before I left for the day. Breakfast tomorrow in the Breakfast Room 7:30?*

Bea's chest tightened. *You were going to do this to help Sarah, remember?* Bea returned her cup to the table decisively. This mystery wasn't going to solve itself. If she was going to help her sister, then she needed to start piecing together the clues despite how out of her depth she felt. *Come on, Bea. You've seen the TV shows. Motive, means, and opportunity.*

She leaned over and grabbed her laptop from the other side of the coffee table. The screen flickered to life, lighting up the room with its brightness. She opened a new document, then with her fingers hovering over the keys, she hesitated. *Where do I start?*

She mumbled to herself, "Every crime needs a victim, doesn't it?"

She typed into the document, creating a heading in each column: Sarah; Francis Court; Posh and Fabulous; Lucinda. Then she gave the first row a title: Reason. *Alright, this is working.*

She clicked her tongue. *So why would each of these be a potential target?* Under the heading 'Sarah', she typed: 'Personal grudge? Professional jealously?'

Who would want Sarah to fail? Everyone loved Sarah, didn't they? But Bea knew she still needed to consider the option. She needed to ask Sarah if there was anyone she'd upset recently. *That's going to be a fun conversation!*

She moved onto 'Francis Court'. That would have to be about reputation. She wrote that, then added: 'Rival? Competitors?' Perhaps someone stood to benefit from fewer events being hosted at the estate. She would have to ask Sarah if any other venues were vying for the same high-profile clients.

Bea absently stroked Daisy's head as she moved to the next column. 'Posh and Fabulous'. Had the catering company made enemies in the cutthroat world of luxury event planning? She jotted down, 'Talk to Sarah/P&F staff re:inside drama or staff grudges'. Her mind flashed to the head chef, Nat Harper, and his devastated face. But had that been real shock or Oscar-worthy acting? He certainly had means and opportunity to have damaged the cake. But what about the other incidents? She shrugged and opened a new sheet in the document. She wrote 'Suspects' at the top and typed in Nathan's name.

Returning to the previous sheet, she moved to the column with Lucinda's name. Now there was someone it was easy to believe could have left a trail of ruffled feathers in her wake. Even Sarah, who was much more measured than Bea, was hardly president of the Lucinda fan club. "Who might have it in for the birthday girl?" she asked under her breath as she typed. Again, she recalled the detective shows Sam subjected her to; didn't they always say that if you wanted to catch the killer, you needed to get to know the victim first? *Except Lucinda hasn't been murdered*, she reminded herself. *Well, hopefully, the principle still stands.* It seemed believable that Lucinda could've upset someone involved in organising her birthday party over the last week. She'd ask Sarah. *And maybe*, she thought, *I'll give cousin Sophie a ring and see what she's got to say about Lucinda for a bit of background.*

She leaned back and looked at the document with satisfaction. This was coming along. Her fingers hovered over the keyboard again, a frown creasing her brow. "Access," she muttered to herself. She typed 'Ask Adrian Breen'. Francis Court's head of security could tell her who had been on the property when each incident had occurred. Suddenly, she stopped, her hand frozen in mid-air. *Wait.* When *had* these crimes actually been committed? She leaned back, pinching her lips together. She would need to know that *before* she could cross reference it with whoever had been on-site.

She created a new sheet, labelling the columns: Guest

List; Centrepiece; and Cake. Along the rows, she typed, 'Timeline?' She needed to work on that one. Underneath, she wrote, 'How?' Under 'Cake,' she typed, 'Bashed in with a saucepan'. *That one is straightforward enough.* The other Hows were trickier. She'd no idea what had caused the decoration to collapse or when the original guest list had last been seen. More questions to add to her growing list.

Bea sat back, rather pleased with her progress. She had the start of a solid investigation here, if she did say so herself. She saved the document and shut her laptop with a satisfying *click*. Her mouth was dry, so she took a sip of her now cold tea. *Can I do this after all?* It was simply a process of elimination, wasn't it?

Famous last words, she thought wryly. Her chest fluttered. *I'll do this. For Sarah's sake.* And perhaps a little bit to prove to herself that she could…

9

EARLY MORNING. THE DAY BEFORE THE PARTY...

Sitting in the Breakfast Room, Perry sipped his coffee, his eyes darting to the door leading to the kitchen. The aroma of freshly baked croissants wafted through the air, making his stomach growl. Where was their food?

At that moment, Lady Beatrice breezed in, her red hair swinging. She sailed right past their table without so much as a glance their way. Perry frowned as she joined Sarah at a table across the room.

"How rude," he muttered. "Not even a hello."

Claire Beck followed his gaze. "Do you know her then?"

Perry stuck his chin out. "Well, not exactly. But I'm working for her sister. She must know who I am," he replied, smarting.

Claire rolled her eyes, then said, "It's unusual to see Lady Beatrice in here though."

"She's sticking her snooty nose into our party planning, I'll bet," Perry sniped, watching Bea and Sarah chatting in the corner.

"They might simply be having breakfast together. Because, you know, they're sisters, Perry." Claire smirked.

"Sounds like someone's jealous to me. Are you worried she'll usurp your new position as Sarah's right-hand man?"

Perry bristled. "Hardly. Lady Beatrice doesn't know the first thing about running a house like this. She's never shown the slightest interest."

"That's a bit unfair, don't you think? For a start, it's not her job. And also, she does have a young son to look after on her own."

Perry shrugged irritably. *A son who's at school most of the day!* Perry's retort died on his lips as their food arrived. He stabbed at his eggs. He couldn't work out what was bothering him so much. But something about Lady Beatrice's sudden interest in Lucinda's party was rubbing him up the wrong way. Was it because she was an unknown variable, liable to muck up all his carefully laid plans?

Claire set down her fork, her expression shifting to one of amusement. She tilted her head, her curly brown hair falling in front of her eyes. She quickly pushed it out of the way. "It's lovely to see you, as always, but I get the distinct impression there's something specific you need from me. Out with it."

Perry flashed her a sheepish grin. *She's too perceptive by half.* He held his hands up in front of his chest. "You've got me. I'm hoping you might have some insight into any... er, disgruntled employees who might want to cause trouble here."

"Trouble?" Claire frowned. "What sort of trouble?"

Leaning in, Perry lowered his voice conspiratorially and told her about the disruptive incidents that had occurred over the last few days. He finished with, "I'm worried someone may be trying to sabotage the event."

Claire's eyes widened. "Goodness, really?" She tapped her finger against her lips, thinking. "Well, there's Greg

Morton from maintenance. Sarah filed a complaint about him recently for neglecting repairs. We only had an informal chat with him about it, but he took it quite badly…"

Perry's pulse quickened. That would certainly explain Greg's hostile attitude yesterday. And as a member of the maintenance team, Greg had access to all areas of the estate. *Means, opportunity, and motive!* He immediately shot to the top of Perry's suspect list.

Hold on though. "So it wasn't a proper disciplinary warning?" Perry clarified.

Claire shook her head.

Would he really risk getting caught and losing his job just to get back at Sarah?

Claire answered that for him when she added, "He'd be an idiot to cause trouble and make it formal."

Perry's shoulders slumped. "I don't suppose anyone else springs to mind?"

"Not off the top of my head, but I'll check the records when I get to the office and let you know if anything stands out."

"Great. I have another small favour…"

"Shoot!"

"Can you find out for me who was on-site on these days during these times?" He slipped a piece of paper across the table to her.

She glanced down at it. "Maybe…" she replied, looking up at him, her head tipped to one side and a glint in her eye. "What's it worth?"

Perry smirked. "How about some of Simon's Italian butter cookies?" *Simon won't mind, will he? He said he'd help me…*

From the dreamy look on Claire's face, he knew he had her.

"Okay. It's a deal. Leave it with me, and I'll get back to you later this morning."

"Thanks, Claire." Perry reached over and squeezed her hand gratefully.

"You're welcome." She smiled as she rose. "I hope it goes well tomorrow night," she said as she gathered her phone and keys off the table and left.

Perry cast a final suspicious glance at Lady Beatrice, who was drinking coffee while Sarah demolished her food. He looked down at his empty plate and huffed. *I bet she's one of those people that doesn't eat!*

He left the restaurant via the back entrance and walked down the corridor and past the various rooms until he got to the office that had been assigned to Posh and Fabulous for them to use.

The door was ajar. He pushed it open. "Hello?"

Empty.

Perry's jaw clenched. *After everything that's happened, how can they be so careless?*

At that moment, Evie bustled in, a takeaway cup in her hand. "Oh! Perry! Sorry, I only popped out to the Old Stable Block Cafe to get a coffee."

"Evie," Perry said, fighting to keep his voice calm. "You really need to lock up when no one's here."

She waved a dismissive hand. "Someone's always around."

Always? Well, where are they now then?

He bit his tongue. He'd made his point. His eyes roamed the office. "So have the party favours arrived yet?" He mentally crossed his fingers.

Evie nodded, her sleek bob swaying. "Yes, they came in late yesterday afternoon. The only thing left is to add the name tags." She gestured to a stack of boxes by the desk. "Black bags for the gentlemen, teal for the ladies."

Relief washed over Perry. *Thank goodness.* They should've been here two days ago, and he'd begun to get paranoid that the goodies had been purposely delayed.

As Perry turned to leave, a man poked his head in the doorway. "Evie, could you come and look at the social media corner? I want to make sure it's set up the way you want."

"Of course, I'll be right there," Evie replied briskly. She flashed Perry an apologetic smile. "I'll get the bags labelled later this morning, okay? I must dash."

Before Perry could agree and remind her once again to lock up, she was gone, the click of her heels echoing down the hall.

He shook his head ruefully. Evie was nothing if not efficient. He looked over to where she'd pointed out the boxes of favours. *Sarah would like to see one, wouldn't she?* And it would be a little reassurance that something, at least, was on track. He walked over, and selecting a black organza bag at random, he tucked it under his arm and strode out.

10

BACK AT BREAKFAST. THE DAY BEFORE THE PARTY...

Bea strolled across the black-and-white chequered marble floor of the Painted Hall and turned right at the Salon to enter the Breakfast Room from the back entrance. As she pushed open the door of the restaurant, the aroma of sickly sweet pastries mingled with salty bacon made her stomach turn. *How can anyone eat this early in the morning?* Bile rose in her throat as her eyes desperately roamed the room that buzzed with the quiet chatter of the staff preparing for another busy day at Francis Court.

She spotted her sister over in the far corner and swallowed. *If I can just get to her and sit down, this will pass.* A legacy from her pregnancy with Sam, Bea couldn't face food until she'd been up for at least three hours and had drunk a gallon of coffee. She'd rarely eaten breakfast in ten years. *I need a coffee!* Totally focussed on getting to where her sister was, she weaved her way through the tables and chairs, oblivious to everything else around her.

"Sorry I'm late," Bea mumbled as she threw herself into the chair opposite Sarah and let out a deep breath. "I couldn't find Sam's rugby boots."

Sarah looked up from her eggs Benedict and nodded towards a pot in the middle of the table. "I ordered you coffee," she said through a mouthful of food.

Bea dived on the pot immediately, pouring herself a large steaming black coffee, and took a gulp. *Ah...* Her shoulders relaxed as the bitter drink slipped down her throat. *And breathe...* As she leaned back in her chair, she eyed her sister as she delicately cut into her poached egg, the yolk oozing onto the ham and toasted muffin beneath. She looked away. An empty feeling in the pit of her stomach opened up, and it wasn't hunger. *How am I going to ask Sarah if she's angered anyone enough recently that they might want to ruin her party plans?* Bea took another sip of coffee, buying time as Sarah looked up. Their eyes met.

"Is everything alright, Bea? You seem… er, nervous."

Bea set down her cup with a soft *clink.* "Sarah, I need to ask you something, and I'm not quite sure how to put it."

Sarah's fork paused midway to her mouth. "Oh?"

Bea inhaled deeply. *Say it!* "Have you... upset anyone recently?" The words tumbled out in a rush.

Sarah's eyes widened. "Have I… What?" She blinked rapidly, her beautifully shaped eyebrows drawing together.

Bea's cheeks warmed. "I'm sorry… That came out all wrong… I meant—"

Sarah held up her hand, cutting her off. "No, no. I see where you're going with this." She dabbed at her lips with a napkin, her composure returning. "You're wondering about all the… incidents and if someone is trying to ruin this for me?"

Bea leaned forward. "Indeed," she whispered. "So is there anyone who could be out to get you?"

Sarah's gaze grew distant for a moment, then she pulled a

face. "Well, now that you mention it, there was some business with Greg Morton."

Bea tilted her head to one side. "Who's Greg?"

"Really, Bea?" her sister scolded. "You should make more of an effort to get to know the staff here."

That's harsh! Bea leaned back and crossed her arms. "Well, it's not really my job to—"

"He's one of the maintenance team," Sarah cut in. "He's been here for years."

Before Bea could further her point that unlike her sister, she had no official role at Francis Court, and therefore had no need to know all the staff, Sarah continued, "Anyway, we had a… er, disagreement last week about some repairs that should have been done. He felt I was pushing him too hard, but honestly, the man's been slacking lately. I spoke to Alex, his boss, and I believe HR got involved. The feedback I got was that Greg hadn't been happy that he'd been reprimanded even though it'd only been an informal chat."

Bea forgot about Sarah's rebuke, her curiosity piqued. "So do you think he was so cross, he might have taken revenge?"

Sarah patted the back of her hair. "I can't imagine him doing that." She sighed. "But I suppose it's possible."

Bea nodded, then asked, "Anyone else?"

Sarah leaned back, her brows furrowed. "No, but Perry did say he would find out who was doing it and stop them. Which was sweet of him."

Sweet? Bea hesitated. Sarah's new assistant seemed very keen to help. Did he just want to go the extra mile to impress his boss, or did he have his own agenda? *Is he really being sweet? Or is he simply playing a clever game…*

Bea looked around the room for the first time since she'd arrived. *Is that Perry over there talking to a woman with curly hair?* He reached over to the woman and squeezed her hand, then she rose and walked away. Perry straightened and turned in her direction. Bea swiftly grabbed her coffee cup and raised it to her mouth. As she took a sip of lukewarm coffee, she could feel his eyes on her. *Is he trying to eavesdrop on our conversation?* She looked up, prepared to meet his stare, but he'd already turned around and was heading for the door. *I've got your number, Perry, Mr Perfect Executive Assistant!*

Opposite her, Sarah was finishing her plate of food. Back to business. She still had questions to ask. "So, er, Sarah, is there anyone who would feel threatened about what you're doing here on the events side? A local rival, perhaps?"

Sarah tipped her head, the corners of her mouth turning downwards. "The whole county of Fenshire is littered with stately homes, but they concentrate mainly on public events rather than private ones. And the hotels in King's Town and Fawstead do weddings and parties but not on this scale. So, no, I don't think so."

Bea mentally crossed that reason off her list. She glanced at her phone. *Is that the time?* She needed to be quick. She had to take the boys to school. *What else did I want to ask her?* She wished she'd printed off the document last night as she racked her brain. *Ah, Posh and Fabulous!* "What about P&F? Any rival competitors or internal issues there?"

Sarah laid her knife and fork across her empty plate. "Not that I'm aware of. They have quite a unique offering. And to be honest, I think their prices separate them from other party planners in the area, which is why most of their clients are in London. As to internal issues. I don't think there are any. Although…" She paused, her brown eyes narrowing. "I had to make a complaint about the cleaning after the last party. But it's all sorted now."

Okay. Not massively helpful. Next? Timeline...

Bea leaned forward, her green eyes intent. "The list of guests, Sarah. When did you last see it before it disappeared?"

Sarah's fingers drummed on the table as she stared absently into space. "Let's see... I definitely had it on my clip-board towards the end of the day because I remember double-checking it before I left."

"In your office?"

"No." Sarah shook her head. "I was in the Red Ballroom at the time. I think I put it down on the sideboard in there and then forgot about it. Perry told me he'd picked it up when he'd finished in there an hour or so later and had put it back in my office."

Bea's mind raced. *Perry again!* But then, if Sarah had left it lying around in the Red Ballroom…

"So anyone could've taken the list off," she murmured.

Sarah's eyes widened. "I suppose so. I hadn't thought of that."

Bea glanced at her phone again, suppressing a sigh. "I've got to run. The boys need to get to school."

As Bea rose, Sarah caught her arm. "Give my boy a hug from me," she said with a sigh. Bea nodded and smiled before hurrying off to collect Sam before she was late getting him and Robbie to school.

11

NOT THAT LONG AFTER. THE DAY BEFORE THE PARTY…

In Sarah's office, Perry proudly presented the favour bag. "What do you think?"

She glanced up at him from her computer. "Very swanky," she said. "I'll take a look at it when I've finished this."

She went back to typing as he mumbled, "Of course," and placed it on the edge of her desk before retreating from the room.

In his own office, Perry tapped Greg Morton's name into his phone. Greg Morton was still his prime suspect. His only suspect right now. Greg had motive, means, and opportunity. If he'd been on-site for the other incidents, then—

The door flew open. Sarah stormed in, her face like thunder. She hurled the party bag onto his desk.

"Is this some kind of sick joke?"

Perry blinked, bewildered. "What? No, I—"

Sarah groaned. "Oh, heck! You don't know, do you?"

Perry's stomach churned. "Know what?"

"Look inside the bag," she said, crossing her arms.

With trembling hands, Perry tipped it up from its end and emptied the bag. The contents clattered onto his desk—a gold-plated tie clip, a Swarovski crystal bottle stopper, some gourmet coffee sachets, a Chanel lip balm, luxury chocolate truffles, an engraved pen commemorating Lucinda's party... He stared down at the expensive pile of items. *Is that a bronze Arc pulse iPhone cover? Wow!* "I don't understand," he stammered. "These are amazing. It must have cost a fortune for a hundred and twenty—"

Then he saw it. A slip of paper. *Wait...* Wasn't there supposed to be a card with an inspirational quote on it? He'd seen a mock-up copy, hadn't he? What had it said? *Something cheesy like, 'Class is timeless, just like you'.* It was supposed to be printed on high-quality card stock, not a cheap scrap of paper. *Oh no...*

Sarah's voice was ice. "Read it."

Perry's throat went dry as he read aloud, "You're only here because your mother begged for an invite." The blood drained from his face. What the—

"They'll all need checking, Perry."

He nodded slowly, letting the paper slip from his fingers. "Leave it with me. I'll get it sorted."

"I need *you* to do it. I don't trust anyone else," Sarah insisted. "Bring them all here. Take everything out of each one. Check them all. Every single one. Forget about putting the cards in unless you can find them easily. They were awfully cheesy anyway. Then lock the bags up in *here*. Okay?"

Perry nodded, his heart sinking. "Right. Of course."

Five minutes later, as he hurried towards the events office, he silently prayed. *Please, let it just be this one. One rogue bag. Not all of them.* But deep down, he knew better.

Back in his office, he meticulously inspected each bag. His hopes plummeted with every nasty message he uncovered.

Fake it 'til you make it—but you'll never make it.

His hands were getting damp as he rummaged in the next bag.

Mirror, mirror on the wall… Oh wait, don't look.

He sighed. A fleeting admiration for the person who'd made these all up passed over him.

Some people are born great; others have to fake it. Guess which one you are?

They were nasty, insulting… and yet quite witty.

If you think you're classy, you should raise your standards.

But this was clearly another attempt at sabotage.

Try not to embarrass yourself too much tonight. Oh wait, too late.

With a sigh, he dropped the last slip of paper into the bin by his side. *Done.* Well, not exactly. He picked up an envelope that was on the corner of his desk and tipped out a list with names and either B or T written by the side, along with a pile of beautifully handwritten gift tags. He still had to attach the tags to the right colour bag. Someone from Posh and Fabulous should be doing this, but he couldn't risk it.

And to be extra careful, he would check every name and make sure the allocation of black or teal bags was correct. He couldn't take any chances.

12

MEANWHILE...

Bea's fingers drummed against the leather seat as Ward, her driver, navigated the winding country roads to take them back home. The boys' chatter from the outward journey had now been replaced by the hum of tires on asphalt. Daisy sat with her head on Bea's leg, gently snoring. Bea re-ran through the earlier conversation with her sister. All she'd really learned was that anyone could have taken the guest list, and a member of the maintenance team *could* be angry with Sarah after he'd got a telling off. It was hardly earth-shattering, was it? Suddenly, a thought struck her. Ward also did some handyman-type maintenance when he wasn't chauffeuring the family around or looking after the estate's fleet of vehicles. *Perhaps he can provide some useful insight...*

She leaned as far forward as she could, unsuccessfully trying not to disturb Daisy, who moved with a huff, turning her back on Bea as she curled up on the leather seat beside her. "Er, Ward?"

He glanced into his rearview mirror and caught her eye. "Yes, my lady?"

"What do you know about Greg Morton? I believe he works in the maintenance department."

The older man's gloved hands tightened on the steering wheel. "Worried sick about that fallen decoration, he is. Can't say I blame him."

Bea started. Why was Greg worried about the decoration centrepiece? Unless of course… "Was he the one who installed it?"

He nodded solemnly. "He swears blind it was secure when he put it up."

"And is he ever careless?"

"Greg? Lord, no, my lady. Reliable as the sunrise, that one. But…" Ward's voice trailed off.

"But what?"

Ward sighed. "He's been under a lot of stress lately. His wife's ill, you see. Very ill. Probably not got long. He's been caring for her at home."

Bea's heart sank. *Oh no, that's awful. I wonder if Sarah knows*. She frowned. "That must be difficult."

"Aye. His daughter thinks she needs to go into a care home. Greg, though, he's stubborn and won't hear of it." Ward glanced back at Bea. "He says he doesn't want to give up on her."

Bea bit her lip, a pang of sympathy welling up inside her. "Could the stress have caused him to make a mistake with the decorations?"

Ward's eyes met hers in the mirror, his gaze firm. "Greg's the most careful guy I know. He might be behind schedule, but he's meticulous. He told me himself he double-checked those bolts. I believe him."

"Then what could've happened?" Bea asked, more to herself than to Ward.

"Well," he said, slowing for a turn. "That scaffold platform was up for the rest of the day after Greg had finished that morning. The events team needed it to put up their crystal doodahs and fairy lights, so anyone could've tampered with it, my lady. Loosen a few bolts, and it's just a matter of time before gravity does the rest."

Bea sat back, her mind churning over this new information. That was *another* incident when anyone who'd been around could be the culprit. Maybe her next errand would help narrow it down. They were approaching the main gates to the estate. "Can you drop me at the security office, please, Ward? I need to speak with Adrian Breen."

"Of course, my lady."

As they pulled up at the front of the security block, Bea's hand was already on the door handle. "Thank you, Ward. You've been incredibly helpful." She gently nudged Daisy. "Come on, sleepy head. Let's go."

Forty minutes later, as Bea made her way back through the house to her apartment via the back stairs, a white blur careered out of the catering kitchen, nearly bowling her over. She stumbled, catching herself against the wall as Daisy barked at the figure disappearing down the corridor.

"What in the world?" Bea muttered, smoothing herself down. She scooped up the little terrier in her arms and gingerly pushed open the door to the kitchen. It was chaos inside. Pots clanged, steam billowed, and in the centre of it all, stood Nat, the burly chef, looking utterly frazzled.

"My lady," he exclaimed, his face pale. "I'm so sorry. We're in a bit of a state here."

Bea's heart sank. *What now?* She tightened her grip on Daisy, who had started to fidget.

Nat ran a hand through his thinning hair. "My team are dropping like flies. Upset stomachs apparently. That was the third to rush out in ten minutes," he continued, pointing to the door.

Another chef stood nearby, looking distinctly green. "Are you alright?" Bea asked with concern.

"I'm fine," he croaked unconvincingly.

Bea turned to Nat. "Could it be something they've eaten?"

"We've been prepping tomorrow's starters," Nat explained, gesturing to an array of half-finished dishes.

"Is there anything they've eaten or tasted that you haven't?" she asked.

Nat frowned. "We taste everything as we go along." He paused. "Except I haven't got around yet to—"

A retching sound stopped him in his tracks as the chef who Bea had addressed earlier pointed to a silver metal container, then slapped his hand over his mouth and ran out of the room.

Nat's eyes widened as he watched the man leave, then he mumbled, "The hollandaise? I made it yesterday, but…" He grabbed the container, sniffing it. "It must have gone off."

Before Bea could stop him, Nat upended the sauce into the sink. "Wait!" she cried, but it was too late. Someone had tampered with it, she was sure. She clenched her jaw. *But now it's too late to prove it!* Had Nat deliberately sabotaged the food, and that was why he was so keen to wash away the evidence? But then, all this was going to do was create more work for him. And now he was without his team to help him. *It seems unlikely.* But if not him, then who?

"Nat," she said to the chef, who was swilling out the container with water. "When exactly did you make that sauce?"

"Er, yesterday, around four, I think. I put it straight in the fridge afterwards," he replied as he placed it in the pile of other unwashed equipment by the side of the sink.

"And no one touched it until this morning?"

Nat shrugged. "As far as I know. We got in at about eight. Why?"

Bea filed away the information. "Just curious. What about the cake that got destroyed? When did you bring that in?"

"Oh, that was the day before. About three, I guess."

"And is the kitchen locked overnight?" Bea asked, trying to keep her voice casual.

Nat shook his head. "Not that I know of."

Bea's mind raced. Another piece of the puzzle to add to the overall picture.

Nat frowned. "Do you think someone has been tampering with things in here?"

Bea gave him a noncommittal look. "Do you know of any reason someone would want to—"

Suddenly, the kitchen doors burst open. A slim woman with a sleek bob strode in, her face a mask of barely contained fury. Daisy wriggled to get down so she could greet the newcomer. Bea held her closer. "Not in the kitchen," she whispered to the little white dog. She probably shouldn't have brought her in here in the first place. *I'd best take her out before I get in trouble.*

"Evie," Nat said weakly.

Bea recognised the name as she inched towards the door. *This must be Evie Hayes from Posh and Fabulous.* Sarah had mentioned her yesterday. Bea edged closer towards the exit as Evie, who didn't seem to have noticed Bea and her attempt to hide Daisy in her arms, rounded on Nat. "How is all of this going wrong on your watch, Nat? First the cake, now this?"

Good question, Bea thought as she slipped out of the

room. She stopped and leaned down to let Daisy jump out of her arms and onto the floor.

"Is this about Jas?" Evie's voice rose. "Because if so, you need to get over it, or you'll lose your job. Is that what you want?"

Bea paused outside the open door, her curiosity piqued. *What does Jas have to do with anything?* Perhaps there was something going on at Posh and Fabulous that Sarah wasn't aware of?

Nat's voice came back, defensive and pleading. "I'm a great chef! Someone's doing this to make me look bad!"

"If you think you're a great chef" —Evie's voice dripped with disdain— "then you're delusional!"

Bea winced. That seemed unnecessarily harsh. She heard footsteps approaching and quickly scurried away, Daisy close behind, her mind whirling with new questions and suspicions.

13

TEN MINUTES LATER...

Bea burst into her apartment on the second floor of Francis Court, Daisy hot on her heels. She shut the door behind her and took in a deep breath. Daisy trotted over to a water bowl in the hallway and was soon lapping at it noisily. Bea strode into the butler's pantry off the entrance and got a glass of water for herself, then hurried into the sitting room, keen to get everything she'd seen and heard into her document before she forgot any of it. She grabbed her laptop from the table and flipped it open before lowering herself onto the edge of the sofa. Daisy jumped up next to her and, after circling twice, found a comfy spot and curled up.

Her laptop whirred to life. Bea's fingers flew across the keyboard, updating her investigation document with frantic energy. She added the tampered sauce to her list of incidents, muttering under her breath as she worked. "Sauce made at four. Kitchen possibly unlocked overnight. In at eight next morning; staff ill within an hour." She then added the timelines for the remaining events.

She leaned back, rubbing her temples. Now she needed to cross-reference it with her own notes from her chat with

Adrian. She took out her phone, opened up her note's app, and transferred the information into the document.

Her phone beeped, causing her to pause. *Sarah.* She opened it.

Sarah: *It never ends! Slips of paper have been added to the party favours with insulting messages on them...*

The muscles in Bea's neck went rigid. *What?* She quickly typed a reply, asking when it had happened. Sarah replied that it had been sometime between four yesterday afternoon and nine this morning. The bags had been left, unlocked in the temporary events office used by Posh and Fabulous. *Another unlocked room that anyone could have got into!*

Bea: *Hate to state the obvious, but I think you need to start locking rooms until after the event.*

Sarah: *Yes. I'm on it.*

She suddenly realised Sarah hadn't mentioned the situation with the chefs being ill. Does she know yet? Bea's throat burned. She sipped some water. *I don't want to be the one to tell her!* But someone had to.

Bea: *Are you aware that a few of the chefs who were prepping food for tomorrow have taken ill? Nothing serious. Evie is on top of it with Nathan, the head chef.*

Bea waited, but no immediate response came. *She's probably already on her way to the kitchen.*

Bea added the party bags incident and timeline to her sheet and checked how it affected the list she'd got from Adrian Breen. Finally, she finished typing. Her tummy fluttered as her eyes narrowed, and she read the list of names of those who'd been on-site during the timeline of all five sabotage attempts.

Greg Morton. The maintenance man who had installed the fallen centrepiece. Under pressure with a sick wife and possibly upset with Sarah for having reported him to his boss.

Evie Hayes. The fiery woman from the kitchen. She clearly wasn't happy with Nat. But why?

Nat Harper, the chef. Was he a convenient scapegoat? And what was going on between him and Jas from Posh and Fabulous?

Next was a name Bea didn't know. Sally Wells. According to Adrian, she worked for one of the contractor cleaning companies employed by Posh and Fabulous. Hadn't Sarah said something about having made a complaint about the cleanup after the last event? Could that be connected in some way?

And finally there was Perry Juke. He'd been around for all the incidents according to the information Adrian had given her. He hadn't been on her original list, but she couldn't ignore that he'd had opportunity and probably means. But what could be his motive? Was he really as efficient and reliable as Sarah seemed to think? Or was he up to no good? Suddenly a thought struck her. What if Sarah's new assistant had been staging these disasters so he could then swoop in and save the day? A would-be hero… *Was that too ridiculous?* She grinned. *Er, probably…* It seemed extreme, but she couldn't totally dismiss him. Not yet.

She looked at the five names. *My suspects!* She shifted in her chair. "It has to be one of you," she said aloud. "But which one?"

14

THE AFTERNOON BEFORE THE PARTY…

Perry strode down the corridor, his polished boots clinking against the hardwood floor. *Which one of them is it?* Having attached labels to the correct party favours, Perry had taken a break and updated his notes with the information Claire had sent him about everyone's whereabouts during the incidents. He now had three main suspects: Greg Morton, from maintenance; Nat Harper, the chef; and Sally Wells, the cleaner. All had been on-site at the relevant times, including the most recent tampering with the sauce in the kitchen that Sarah had told him about earlier. Of course, Evie Hayes had also been around when all the incidents had taken place, but he couldn't imagine why she would want to cause trouble any more than he would. It would be pointless. After all, it was their job to make sure it all went smoothly.

Perry had initially thought Greg the most likely, but Claire had made a good point at breakfast. Would he risk getting caught and possibly losing his job because of a telling off? *It seems unlikely.* So for now, he would concentrate on Nat and Sally. He knew very little about them, hence why he was on his way to the events office. Both worked for Posh and Fabulous. And although Sally seemed an unlikely suspect as she'd nearly been wiped out by the falling centre-piece, for the moment, he would keep an open mind and see what he could find out. He was hoping Evie could shed some light on why either of them would want to cause all this trouble.

As Perry breezed into the office, the party planner glanced up from her laptop, her hazel eyes narrowing. "Why did you take the party favours?" she asked, her tone clipped.

Hello to you too! "Lady Sarah's orders. She wanted to keep them locked away. They're very valuable, and there are a lot of people coming and going in this part of the building."

He and Sarah had agreed not to say anything to anyone about having found the notes in the bags. The fewer people who knew about the attempts to disrupt the birthday celebrations, the better.

Evie's brow furrowed. "That's all very well, but the labels still need adding. I was going to get my team—"

"Already done," Perry said with a smug smile. "You can tick that off your list."

Her lips pursed. Perry could sense her annoyance, but really, it was her own fault. She was the one who'd been lax with office security. However, it was clear he wasn't going to get much out of her if she was mad at him. He needed to thaw her out.

"We've both been so busy today." He flashed her a smile. "I think we deserve a break, don't you?"

A flicker of surprise crossed Evie's face. She raised an eyebrow.

"Why don't I treat you to afternoon tea in the restaurant? It's to die for…"

A tentative smile tugged at the corners of her mouth. *Come on! You know you want to…*

"I skipped lunch, so… yes, that would be lovely, actually."

Perry beamed at her and gestured to the door. "After you."

Twenty minutes later, Perry took a huge bite of lemon tart as he watched Evie devour a miniature cheese scone in one go. Her demeanour appeared to be softening. The Breakfast Room's elegant ambiance and the delectable spread before them had worked their magic. Time to start his investigation. "I was surprised to see Sally Wells cleaning up yesterday only a few hours after she'd had a near miss with the falling decoration. That was very dedicated of her…" he said. "Has she worked for P&F for long?"

She dabbed her lips with a napkin. "She doesn't actually work for P&F directly. We subcontract the cleaning to a third party. She works for them. But…" She hesitated.

Perry leaned in. "But…?"

"Well, I have to say I've been surprised to see her here over the last few days. I thought the cleaning company had sacked her."

Sacked? That's promising….

Evie lowered her voice and continued, "After Lady Sarah complained about the shoddy cleaning job they did at the last event."

Perry's eyebrow slowly crept up his forehead. *Sarah?* Was this about Sarah and not Posh and Fabulous? "And was Sally responsible for that?"

She shrugged. "I assumed so, since she was here cleaning for that event."

It didn't seem like Evie knew any more about it. He'd

have to do a bit more digging. But at least he now had a possible motive for Sally.

He picked up a delicate smoked salmon blini. "So what's it like working for P&F, Evie?"

Her face held a blank expression. "It's… fine," she said, her voice guarded.

Only fine? "Come on," Perry coaxed, leaning in conspiratorially. "Jas must be quite the inspiration, achieving so much so young."

Evie snorted, then quickly covered her mouth. "Sorry, it's... Well, it's her parents' company, you know. She and her sister Holly run it for them."

"Ah." Perry nodded sagely. "That explains her entitled air then."

The party planner relaxed visibly, a small smile playing at her lips. "Holly's the real brains," she said. "Jas…. Well, she looks good and barks orders."

Perry chuckled. "Yeah, I can picture that. And how do the staff feel about working there?"

Evie took a sip of her Earl Grey. "Everyone loves Holly," she said, then hesitated. "Jas, though... Well, she's not as popular. Except with some of the men, if you catch my drift."

The side of Perry's mouth quirked upwards. *Interesting…* "Oh? Do tell."

Evie bit her lip. "I really shouldn't…"

"It'll go no further," Perry assured her with a smile. "Promise."

She glanced around furtively before leaning in, her voice dropping to a whisper. "Well, let's just say we have a revolving door of chefs. Jas has a... *thing* for them, if you know what I mean."

Perry's pulse quickened. "Even Nat, the current one?"

"Oh, yes." She nodded. "But she dumped him last week. She does that once she gets bored. He's still fuming about it."

Perry's mind raced. Could this be the motive he was searching for? A jilted lover, wounded pride, only—

"Oh!" Evie squeaked opposite him.

"What is it?" he asked, tilting his head.

Evie hesitated, fidgeting with her teacup. "Well, I've had a thought. After the cake disaster and the kitchen staff falling ill, I can't help wondering if Nat's trying to cause trouble for Jas."

That was what he was thinking. There was only one problem with that. "But wouldn't that be counterproductive? After all, he's the one who has to deal with the fallout."

"I suppose so," she said. "But I know it's causing Jas major headaches. And costing a fortune as well." She lowered her voice further. "They've had to rush-order a new cake at an extortionate price. And they're now paying sick leave for the kitchen staff while also hiring temps to cover. All while trying to keep it hush-hush."

That can't be good for the bottom line.

"Holly and their parents are not happy. It's eating into profits big time."

As they finished their tea, Perry's mind turned over this new development. The new centrepiece must have cost a pretty penny too. What if the goal wasn't to sabotage the event but to drain profits and tarnish Jas's reputation as a capable manager? Nat was looking more suspicious by the minute. He needed to talk to Sarah. They might need to act fast to stop the chef from doing any more damage.

15

TWO HOURS BEFORE THE PARTY...

Bea sipped her coffee as she gazed out of the window of her sitting room. The tree-lined Long Drive, the road that led to The Cascade, a water feature at the front of the house, stretched out into the distance where the imposing main gates could be glimpsed at the far end. As Bea looked down at her laptop screen, the same five names as last night stared back at her. She was ready to wipe Greg Morton off the list. She didn't believe he would jeopardise his job, especially with a sick wife. Last night, she'd passed on to her sister what Ward had told her. At first, Sarah had been upset that Greg had not said anything when he'd been pulled up for getting behind on his jobs. Then she'd immediately promised to talk to HR and arrange compassionate leave of absence for him so he could take care of his wife while he figured out what to do.

Daisy, who was resting her head on Bea's lap, gave a sigh. Bea smiled as she addressed the small terrier. "What do you think, little girl? Which one of the remaining four did it?"

Daisy's tail thumped in response. Bea patted her dog's head. When she and Sarah had discussed the other three of the four names on her list (she'd not been brave enough to bring up Perry's name with her sister), Bea had learned that Sally Wells was a cleaner who'd been given notice following Sarah's complaint about the shoddy clear up of a previous event. They'd agreed that Sally could be angry at Sarah *or* Posh and Fabulous. Either way, it gave her a motive.

Then Sarah had told her about another suspect with a motive. "Evie told Perry that Nat, the chef, and Jas had a fling, but she ended it recently. Now he's furious about it."

Bea had straightened her back as she'd shifted the phone to her other ear. "Is it true or just gossip, do you think?"

"Well, I asked Jas when I had my end-of-day catch-up with her, and she was rather cagey, but she didn't deny it. She said it wasn't a problem and that they were adults who could still work together."

Jas might think that, but did Nat feel the same?

Sarah had continued, "Perry's convinced Nat is behind all the sabotage attempts. It's cost P&F a small fortune to fix all these issues. He might have a point."

Bea had nodded. "Hit her where it hurts, you mean, in terms of money?"

"Jas' parents and her sister, Holly, won't be happy if this party costs more than their fee. It would reflect very badly on Jas and maybe even cause them to rethink her position."

So Nat's Perry's pick, is he? Bea scratched behind Daisy's ears. What Sarah had said last night made sense. But Bea wasn't convinced. She'd seen Nat shortly after he'd discovered the smashed-up cake and again yesterday, when his staff had taken ill. He'd seemed genuinely upset and frustrated. Would he really create all that extra work for himself? Bea's eyes narrowed. It was awfully convenient for Perry to point the finger at Nat. What better way to deflect suspicion from himself than to accuse someone else?

She looked at the list again. That left Evie Hayes. Neither

she nor Sarah had come up with a motive for the party planner to want the party to be a failure. After all, it was her job to make it a success. So as far as Bea could see, it was between Sally, Nat, and Perry as the most likely candidates for saboteur. And at this moment in time, her money was firmly on Perry.

Perry drummed his fingers on Sarah's office desk, his blue eyes darting to the clock on the wall. "We need to confront Nat," he blurted, leaning forward in his chair. "Before he has a chance to sabotage anything else."

Sarah worried her bottom lip with her teeth. "Shouldn't we let Evie do that? She knows him. She'll know how to handle him. It's her event, after all."

Perry waved his hand dismissively. "I've tried calling her. No answer." He stood and pulled down the cuff of his shirt. "We can't afford to wait, Sarah."

"Are you certain Nat's behind all this?" she asked, her tone cautious.

A shiver ran down Perry's spine. *Am I certain?* "He's got an obvious motive, as well as means and opportunity." *More than any of the others.* Sarah had told him first thing that she didn't believe Greg was involved. That only left Sally, the cleaner, and Nat. Sally was still a possibility, of course, but her motive didn't seem as compelling as Nat's. Plus, she almost got crushed by a floral centrepiece. It probably wouldn't have killed her, but would she have taken the risk of walking under it, having known it would fall at some point? "Look, all we need to do is let him know we're onto him," Perry pressed, sensing her hesitation. "If he knows we know, then he'll let it go."

Sarah sighed, rising reluctantly. "Fine. But we must tread carefully. The last thing we need is Nat walking out a few hours before the party begins."

Perry's stomach lurched. *I hope I've got this right...*

———

Bea knew she had to say something to Sarah. If Perry was driving the investigation, then what if he persuaded Sarah to confront Nat? Her sister was at risk of making a total fool of herself. Bea licked her lips. Even worse. *Nat might walk and then...* Was that what Perry was planning? She stood abruptly, startling Daisy from her cosy nest on the sofa. "Come on, Daisy-doo. We need to find Sarah."

The little dog yawned, stretching languidly before hopping down to follow Bea. As they left the apartment, Bea's steps were quick and purposeful. The thought that Perry was setting this all up for his own gain gnawed at her, a persistent itch she couldn't scratch.

As they emerged onto the first-floor landing, a flash of movement caught Bea's eye. A figure pushing a cleaner's trolley disappeared down the east wing corridor. Bea frowned. *Who is that?* She looked at her watch. She was familiar with the routine of the house and knew all the housekeeping staff by sight. It would be unusual for any of them to be on this floor at this time of day. *What are they doing here?* Her chest tightened. With everything going on at the moment, should she be worried?

She turned and tentatively moved towards the east wing corridor. She gazed down the hallway. It was empty. She crept towards the cleaning storeroom at the end, listening for any noise, but all she could hear was Daisy's feet *tap-tapping* on the wooden floor in front of her. "Hello?" she called out.

"Excuse me?" But the corridor was empty; the mysterious cleaner had vanished like smoke.

Bea bit her lip. *Should I investigate further or find Sarah as planned?*

Suddenly, a cry pierced the silence of the first floor. Bea jumped, and Daisy let out a low *woof.* Bea looked around, searching for the source of the noise. Running footsteps made her stop. She listened. It wasn't coming from this corridor. She hurried back to the landing, Daisy trotting at her side. Raised voices and the sound of sobbing caught her attention. It was coming from the west wing. Her heart pounding in her ears, Bea ran.

Perry's pulse sped up as he and Sarah approached the catering kitchen. *This is it.* They'd give Nat a warning shot across the bows, and that would put an end to the sabotage. He, Perry, would save the birthday party. He could almost taste the victory.

"Remember," Sarah said, her slender hand on Perry's arm. "We can't lose him. So no accusations."

Perry nodded, deflating slightly. "Right. Subtle. I can do subtle."

Sarah arched an eyebrow. "Can you?"

Rude! But before Perry could retort, a shout of "Stop!" echoed from behind the kitchen door. Sarah's eyes widened.

Perry's hand flew to the handle.

"Wait—" Sarah started, but Perry had already flung the door open.

The heat and noise inside were overwhelming, a physical presence that caused Perry to step backwards. In the centre of the kitchen stood Nat, his face as red as a tomato, gesticulating wildly at a group of terrified-looking young chefs. "You call that a julienne?" he bellowed, towering over them. "My grandmother could cut straighter than that, and she's been dead for twenty years!"

Perry winced. *I'm not sure this is a good time...*

"This is fine dining, not some motorway cafe!" Nat thundered at his wide-eyed audience. "So if you think this is acceptable, you should raise your standards!" he bellowed. "Everything has to be perfect. It's my reputation on the line! If you lot don't get your act together, this whole thing is going to be a disaster! I won't let you make me look a fool. Do you understand?"

A chorus of, "Oui, Chef!" rang out, the poor youngsters practically quaking in their clogs.

"Now, go—" Nat stopped suddenly, as if he'd only this minute realised someone else was in his kitchen. He whirled around to face Perry and Sarah, his eyes wild. "What do you want?"

The harried-looking sous chefs scurried back to their stations.

Perry opened his mouth. Then closed it. Suddenly, a confrontation didn't seem like such a sensible plan. He looked at Sarah for help, but at that moment, her phone screen lit up. She turned away to deal with it.

"Well?" Nat roared at him.

Bea's heart raced as she hurried down the west wing corridor, Daisy's paws clicking against the polished floor. The cries grew louder, more frantic. She reached an open door and stepped inside, Daisy by her side.

Lucinda Hamilton, resplendent even in her fury, loomed

over a cowering woman. Tears streamed down the poor thing's face as Lucinda's voice cut through the air like a whip. "I don't care if you hung it up yourself!" Lucinda snarled. "That dress cost more than you earn in a year, and now it's gone!"

Bea's eyes darted around the room, taking in two helpless bystanders standing frozen in a corner of the suite.

"I'm so sorry," the crying woman whispered. "It was here thirty minutes ago, I swear." She gave a whimper, and Daisy made a move towards her.

"I don't care—" Lucinda's next words died in a violent sneeze. Her gaze locked onto Daisy as she trotted across the carpet. "Get that mangy mutt out of here!"

Mangy mutt? My Daisy? How dare she! Bristling, Bea rushed forward and scooped up her little terrier. She met Lucinda's glare.

Recognition dawned in Lucinda's eyes. Her demeanour shifted, a saccharine smile replacing the scowl. "Oh, Lady Beatrice! I'm so sorry…" She had the good grace to look a little sheepish.

Bea fought the urge to snap out a reply that it wasn't her Lucinda should be apologising to but the woman she'd made cry. Lucinda was Sarah's client though, and Bea knew of Lucinda's reputation as a diva. *Be nice, Bea.* "Is everything alright?" she asked innocently, pretending she hadn't heard the fuss Lucinda had been making when she'd walked in.

Lucinda's eyes narrowed as she turned back to the woman, who was now wiping her face with her hand. "My dress has disappeared into thin air, it would appear." The women visibly wilted under Lucinda's stare. "And I have a final fitting in—" She checked a diamond-encrusted watch on her right wrist. "Fifteen minutes!"

Bea's mind raced. *Lucinda's gown goes missing just*

before her final fitting. This can't be a coincidence. Someone had taken it deliberately. *But who?* Bea addressed the distressed woman, who she now assumed was a stylist, "When did you last see the dress?"

The stylist blinked, then cleared her throat. "I brought it up when I arrived about thirty-five minutes ago. Miss Hamilton hadn't arrived yet. I hung it up there." She pointed to an empty cream hanger hooked on the outside of a tall wardrobe to her right. She sniffed. "Then I met the others for coffee at the cafe." She glanced over to the other two women, who stood with their arms crossed in the corner. They nodded. "When we got back five minutes ago, the dress was gone."

So someone only had about thirty minutes to take it. How? "Was the suite locked?"

The woman shook her head. "The door was on the latch. There are so many of us coming and going…" She tapered off and gave another sniff. "I wasn't gone for long."

Lucinda huffed loudly. "I don't have time for all this detective work. I need that dress! Where's Sarah?"

Perry's throat burned as he met the angry chef's eyes. He pasted on a smile and straightened up his tall frame. "We wanted to check how things are—"

Nat barked out a harsh laugh. "Well, let's see, shall we? I've lost half my team and been saddled with a bunch of novices. We've been slaving away since dawn, and we're still behind." He threw up his hands. "So things are, er, less than ideal, I'd say, wouldn't you?"

As if to prove his point, a pot clattered to the floor, sending a wave of something red and steaming across the tiles. Nat's attention darted away from Perry as he unleashed a string of curses.

Sarah tugged at Perry's sleeve, her phone in her hand, her face pale. "Perry, we have to go. Now!" she cried above Nat's shouting.

Thank goodness!

Perry let Sarah drag him out of the kitchen and into the hallway. As the door swung shut on the kitchen racket, Perry let out a slow breath. But before he could enjoy the moment of peace, Sarah thrust her phone under his nose. A text glowed on the screen.

Bea: *Lucinda's dress is missing. You're needed ASAP in the Coral Suite.*

16

A FEW MINUTES LATER...

Bea felt a little sick as she watched Lucinda pace the floor of the Coral Suite. *What am I supposed to do?* Should she say something to try to reassure the birthday girl? But what could she say? Lucinda's one-off couture dress had gone missing at Francis Court. There was no way to sugar-coat that. A headache was nagging between her eyes, and Daisy was getting heavier by the second. *Oh, Sarah! Where are you?*

The phone in her hand vibrated. *Sarah!*

Sarah: *On my way!*

Bea's shoulders dropped. Her sister would know what to do. "Lady Sarah is on her way," she said to the room in general.

Lucinda whirled around, her golden hair swinging. "About time! This is a disaster. I can't believe—"

But Bea wasn't listening. A sudden thought had struck her

like a bolt of lightning. "The cleaner," she muttered under her breath.

"What?" Lucinda snapped.

Bea looked up in shock. *Did I say that out loud?* "Er, nothing." She repositioned Daisy in her arms and edged towards the door. "Sarah will be here any minute. In the meantime, please excuse me." Without waiting for a response, Bea bolted out of the room. Gently dropping Daisy down onto the floor, she said, "Come on, Daisy," and walked briskly towards the landing.

A few seconds later, the east wing corridor stretched before her, empty and silent. Her heart thumped loudly as she sped down it and flung open the door to the cleaning storeroom at the end. It was larger than she'd expected, the size of a small bedroom rather than a cupboard. Cleaning trolleys and supplies filled the space. Bea rummaged through the empty bags hanging off the trolleys. Nothing.

Daisy let out a sharp bark. Bea glanced around. No sign of the little dog. *I must have left her outside.*

Bea poked her head around the door. No Daisy in the hallway. Another bark echoed from inside the room.

Bea frowned. "Daisy! Where are you?" she called as she leaned back inside. At the far end of the room, a door she hadn't noticed before swung open with a *thwack*. Out bounded Daisy, her tail wagging.

Bea strolled across the room to greet the excited terrier. "What's in there, Daisy?" She approached the unmarked swing door and gave it a push.

"Finally!" Lucinda's shrill voice cut through the air as Perry and Sarah entered the Coral Suite. She paced like a caged tiger, her golden hair dishevelled from having run her hands through it. "My dress is gone, Lady Sarah. Vanished! This is a nightmare!"

Perry scanned the room, expecting to see Sarah's sister, but the only other people in here were three women huddled in the corner, their faces etched with worry. *They're probably part of Lucinda's entourage,* he thought.

Sarah stepped forward, her voice smooth as silk. "Lucinda, I'm sure it's simply misplaced. We'll find it."

Lucinda whirled on her. "Misplaced? It's a couture gown, not a pair of socks!"

Rude! Sarah was trying to help. Although Perry felt uneasy about her having promised Lucinda that they would find it. If the disappearance of the dress was connected to the other incidents, and he was fairly sure it was, then it was unlikely the gown would be found so easily. They needed a backup plan…

Sarah seemed to read his thoughts. "Do you have an alternative dress?"

"Alternative? But I want *my* dress!" Lucinda's voice rose to a screech.

One woman in the corner timidly raised her hand. "Actually, my lady, there was another dress sent over by the designer. It would look stunning on Miss Hamilton."

Lucinda's eyes narrowed. For a moment, Perry thought she might explode. Then with a huff, she snapped, "Fine. I'll try it. But I want my dress found!"

Sarah turned to Perry. "Would you mind fetching the dress from the hotel in Fawstead where the stylists are staying, please?"

Me? But why can't one of them go? He glanced over at the group of women. One of them scurried forward and handed him a room key. "It's at The Fawstead Inn. Room 205. The dress is red, and it's hanging up in the wardrobe."

Perry gave her a look. *Well, you go then!*

Sarah turned her back so she was facing him, then leaned in and whispered, "I'm sorry, but you're the only one I trust. I'll ask Ward to take you."

Oh, well, in that case... He smiled at the woman and took the key. "Red dress, room 205. I'm on it."

Bea flicked on the light, illuminating the windowless room. Shelves lined the walls, stacked high with pristine towels and neatly folded bedding. *It's a linen closet.* Daisy's eager bark drew her attention.

"What's so exciting, little girl?" Bea asked, watching as Daisy jumped at a flap on the far wall. Bea crossed the room and lifted the flap, revealing a dark chute. "A laundry chute," she murmured, her mind racing. *It must lead to the basement.* She activated the light on her mobile phone, then holding it in front of her, she stuck her head in and peered down. Something caught her eye. Something that sparkled. Her heart quickened. *Could it be?* She tried to get a closer look, but it was lodged just out of reach. She shuffled backwards and pulled her head out through the flap. As she did so, something fell to the floor. She looked down, expecting to see a crystal or button. *No, it looks more like a piece of—*

Before she could finish her thought, Daisy had dived at the morsel of biscuit and gobbled it up. Bea grinned. Well, that explained Daisy's interest in the laundry chute!

Still smiling, she scanned the room for a tool. Nothing.

She dashed back to the cleaning room and snatched up a mop. Returning, she dived through the flap again, her phone in one hand, and plunged the mop handle down the chute with the other.

"Come on, come on," she muttered, fishing for whatever it was stuck in the chute. Suddenly, she felt resistance. With trembling hands, she pulled. As the object emerged, her eyes widened.

A beaded gold gown tumbled out. It was crumpled and creased but intact.

She had goosebumps as she fumbled to switch off the light on her phone. Then with shaky fingers, she texted Sarah.

Perry's polished shoes crunched on the gravel path as he strode towards the garages. His mind buzzed. *Who took the dress?* His mind automatically went to his top suspect—Nat. His stomach clenched. But that didn't seem likely now, did it? He'd seen the chef not that long ago, and he was up to his eyes in food preparation. *Hadn't he said he'd been there since dawn?* It was probably a slight exaggeration, but even so, there was no mistaking Nat's determination to get the food ready on time. It seemed unlikely he would've had the time or, indeed, the inclination to break away from the kitchen, steal the dress, and dispose of it. Perry sighed. *No. Nat is off the list now.*

He spotted Ward, the driver, leaning against a sleek black car and waved at him.

"Ready to go, Mr Juke?" the driver called out.

Perry nodded and sped up. *So that leaves Sally...* Where was that mousy cleaner anyway? Perry hadn't seen her all afternoon.

As he reached for the car door, his phone buzzed.

. . .

Sarah: *Cancel your trip to Fawstead. Bea has found the dress!*

Perry's eyebrows shot up. *Really?* A mixture of relief and curiosity washed over him. *But where?* He turned to Ward, who was hovering by his side, waiting for him to get in the car. "Change of plan, Ward. You can stand down. Thank you." Perry smiled as he turned and headed back the way he'd come. As he trotted towards the house, he couldn't help but wonder how on earth Sarah's disinterested sister had stumbled across the missing dress.

Bea stood in the laundry room, the rescued gown draped over her arm. Daisy sat at her feet, her tail thumping on the floor, looking extremely pleased with herself.

Sarah burst into the room, her eyes wide. "Oh, thank goodness." She rushed over, running her hand over the gown's delicate fabric studded with crystals. "It's wrinkled but nothing a good steaming won't fix."

Bea nodded, a small smile tugging at her lips. "It was stuck in the laundry chute. Daisy here sniffed it out." She paused, then added, "Well, actually, she was after a bit of biscuit that was stuck in the chute. But, well…" She grinned.

Sarah laughed, and bending down, she ruffled the little dog's ears. "Good girl, Daisy!" Then straightening up, she fixed Bea with a curious look. "But how did you know to look here in the first place?"

Bea told her about the mysterious figure with the cleaning trolley. "It was someone I didn't recognise."

Sarah's eyes widened. "And you think they took the dress?"

"The timing fits." Bea shrugged. "So I thought if it *was* the saboteur that I saw, then they could've stashed it somewhere close by. That's why I checked the cleaning cupboard first."

"Did you get a good look at this person?"

Bea shook her head. "I only saw them from the back. They were about my height, slim build, wearing black trousers and one of these logo'd tabards." She pointed to the blue overalls hanging up along the wall. "Anyone could've borrowed one from here, along with a cart."

"Well," Sarah said, tapping her finger against her chin. "That rules out Nat. He's built like a rugby player and is well over six feet."

As is Perry... While waiting for Sarah to arrive, Bea had reluctantly crossed Perry off her suspect list too. *Just as well I never told Sarah about my suspicions of her new assistant.* That could've gone badly!

"And Greg's out too," Sarah continued. "I know we didn't think he was a likely suspect anyway. But I had a message from HR earlier to let me know that they'd sent him home on compassionate leave first thing this morning after they'd spoken to him."

Bea's mind whirred. If it wasn't Nat, Perry, or Greg, then that only left—

Sarah's voice cut through her thoughts. "Right. I need to tell Lucinda the good news, and, of course, find someone to press the dress immediately!" She took the gown from Bea. "You're a lifesaver, sis." She leaned over and planted a kiss on Bea's cheek before heading for the door.

A warmth spread through Bea's body. It felt good to be

useful. She set her jaw. *Now all I have to do is find the person doing this and put a stop to it!*

17

AN HOUR BEFORE THE PARTY…

Bea glanced down at her watch. Only an hour to go before the first guests would arrive for Lucinda's spectacular thirtieth birthday party. She scanned the ornate Red Ballroom at Francis Court, taking in the glittering chandeliers, towering floral arrangements, and the crimson-and-gold drapes adorning the walls. *Sarah and Posh and Fabulous have really outdone themselves.* The room was the embodiment of 'modern-day fairytale', just as Lucinda wanted. And considering the attempts to sabotage the event, it was an amazing feat that it looked so perfect. As if everything had been easy. Bea suppressed a snort. *It's been anything but!*

"Can you believe it's almost time?" Sarah asked, running her hands down the front of her dress. "After all the stress and chaos of the last few days, I need everything to go smoothly tonight."

"It's going to be perfect," Bea replied, tugging at the hem of her long jumper, feeling underdressed amidst the opulence of the Red Ballroom. "And it looks... breathtaking."

Sarah smiled. "Thanks, sis. I just hope Lucinda loves it too." Her smile faltered, and she let out a deep sigh. "And I hope whoever's been causing the chaos has given up. I can't afford any more disasters."

Bea dipped her chin in acknowledgement, her mind racing. *It has to be Sally, doesn't it?* She's the only person left with a motive. *I need to find her.* She would locate and confront the cleaner as soon as she'd checked in on her son. But she wouldn't tell her sister right now. Sarah had enough on her plate focussing on the party without Bea's suspicions adding to it.

Conscious of the time, Bea reached out and squeezed her sister's hand. "I'm going to get on." She pulled a face. "I need to check on Sam. He's supposed to be packing, but you know what ten-year-old boys are like."

Sarah patted Bea's hand in understanding. "Oh, that's right. It's his weekend with James' parents, isn't it?"

Bea's late husband's parents, the Earl and Countess of Durrland, really looked forward to their monthly visits from their only grandson and heir.

"Alright, well, I really must go. Good luck, sis. You've got this." Bea leaned over and hugged her sister before scurrying away. Sam was either lying on his bed, snuggled up with Daisy, and had done nothing since she'd left him half an hour ago, or he was trying to stuff his entire wardrobe into his suitcase.

In the quiet of the back corridor, she allowed herself a moment to breathe. She leaned against the wall, closing her eyes. *Please let tonight go off without any more difficulties.*

18

THIRTY MINUTES BEFORE THE PARTY...

Bea's footsteps were heavy as she climbed Francis Court's ornate main staircase on her way back to her apartment, having seen Sam safely off to his grandparents.

In front of her, Daisy hopped up each step with a lot more vigour than Bea did. *I need a coffee and time to think*. She'd had no luck finding Sally Wells. The cleaner had vanished, it seemed. Plenty of people had seen her this morning, but no one knew where she'd been during the time Lucinda's dress had gone missing. Was she the mysterious maid? Bea hoped so, or else, she was out of options.

As she neared the second floor, voices drifted up from below. Bea halted, recognising Lucinda's plummy tones. And was that... Evie? The event planner? *I hope Lucinda's not complaining about something else that's gone wrong*. But surely, she'd do that directly with Sarah or perhaps Jas? Bea's stomach dropped. Unless she hadn't been able to find them. Bea needed to find out what it was so she could forewarn Sarah.

"Stay!" she whispered to Daisy, then backtracked a few

steps so she could peer through the banister railings without being seen.

There they were. Lucinda, resplendent in her beautiful gold dress, gesticulating with her hands at Evie, who looked tense, clutching her ever-present planner like a shield.

Bea strained to hear, but their words were muffled. Lucinda tossed her golden mane, a practiced smile not quite reaching her eyes. Evie's posture screamed discomfort.

She needed to hear what they were saying. *Oh, I know. I'll pretend I'm on my way down the stairs.* She held her hand up to Daisy to tell her not to move, then, affecting nonchalance, she slowly descended the stairs.

"I expect nothing less than perfection tonight, Evie dear." Lucinda's tone dripped with condescension.

"Of course, Lucinda. Everything is sorted, as I said. Now if you'll excuse me, I need to check… er, on things." Evie backed away, eager to escape. Just as Bea reached the bottom step, the party planner turned and hurried down the stairs.

Rats! That hadn't been very useful. *Oh well, I may as well turn around and head back to my apartment.*

"Oh, Lady Beatrice! I'm so glad I've caught you."

Double rats!

"I must apologise for earlier." A flutter of flawlessly manicured hands accompanied Lucinda's words. "I'm dreadfully allergic to dogs, you see. And I was so distraught about my gown…"

Bea forced a smile. "Of course. No harm done."

"And about that—thank you for locating it so quickly." Lucinda's smile gleamed. "Sarah explained that the maid saw it was a little creased and took it for steaming. I mean, it was very thoughtful, of course, but it would've been useful if she'd told someone."

"Indeed," Bea murmured, impressed by Sarah's quick

thinking. So why had Lucinda been talking to Evie? *Only one way to find out...* "So is everything alright now and on track?"

Lucinda frowned. "Yes, of course. Why do you ask?"

"I couldn't help noticing you talking with Evie," Bea said, trying to keep her tone casual. "So I thought perhaps something was wrong."

A flicker of confusion crossed Lucinda's face before her practiced smile returned. "Oh, that. No. Everything is fine. We were having a little catch-up. We were at school together, you know."

Ah, that explains it then. "Oh, so you're friends? Well, then it must be nice to have your friend here making sure your birthday is—"

Lucinda let out a sharp laugh. "Hardly friends," she scoffed. "She was the year below me and a real dork." She glanced at her diamond-encrusted watch. "Now if you'll excuse me, I really must finish getting ready."

With a swish of fabric, Lucinda was already heading towards the first-floor corridor, leaving only a cloud of expensive perfume.

"Enjoy your party," Bea called after her. Lucinda waved a hand at Bea in return.

As Lucinda disappeared towards her suite, Bea turned and climbed back up the stairs to her apartment, her mind returning to Sally. She really needed to find out one way or another if Sally could be the saboteur.

Five minutes later, with a coffee in one hand, Bea pulled her phone out from the pocket of her jeans with the other and plonked herself down on the sofa. Daisy jumped up to join her. Bea dialled Mrs Crammond's number. The head housekeeper answered on the second ring.

"Hello Mrs Crammond? It's Lady Beatrice. Quick question—do you know where Sally Wells is today?" She inhaled and held her breath as she waited for the answer.

"Sally from the contract cleaners? The girl who almost got crushed by the chandelier a couple days ago? Er, she was here earlier, my lady. We've all been telling her she really should take some time off. She must've had a fright."

What? Could her suspect be the same girl? "Sorry, Mrs Crammond, but can I confirm, please. Sally Wells from Posh and Fabulous is the Sally who was almost hit by the centrepiece decoration in the Red Ballroom?"

"Yes, my lady."

Bother! Why didn't I know that? Maybe Sarah was right. She really needed to spend more time getting to know the staff at Francis Court. She'd hidden herself away since James's death, and had left her sister and mother to run things. With Sam growing up now, maybe she needed to step up and get involved. Not in a public-facing role, of course. She didn't have Sarah's patience or easy manners. *Maybe something behind the scenes?* But for now, was Sally still a viable suspect? She'd hardly take the risk of being in the Red Ballroom if she'd rigged the centrepiece to come down, would she?

The sound of paper rustled down the line. "Ah, here we are. She finished at twelve and isn't due in again until tomorrow morning for the big clean-up."

Bea slowly let the air out through her nose. *So it isn't Sally.*

"Is everything okay, my lady? Do you need some help with anything?"

Yes! You can find out who is doing all these things because I've run out of suspects! "No, Mrs Crammond. Everything's fine. Thank you."

But it's not fine, is it? If Sally wasn't the troublemaker, then who was?

She hung up and fired off a quick text to Adrian Breen. He would be able to confirm Sally's absence on-site this afternoon. *Just in case she was supposed to leave but didn't.*

But as Bea waited for his reply, she felt her confidence deflating like a punctured tyre. She flopped back on the couch. Even if Adrian didn't confirm Sally's absence, her gut was now telling her it wasn't the cleaner. *Clearly, I'm not cut out for this detective lark*, she thought glumly. *What was I thinking, playing Miss Marple?* She buried her face in her hands.

Daisy nuzzled Bea's knee, her tail wagging, then she sighed and rested her head on Bea's lap. Bea removed her hands from her face and stroked Daisy's ears. *I may as well give up.* She was fairly sure from what Sarah had told her that her sister's assistant, Perry, was trying to find out who was responsible. She should leave it to him. But then...

Sarah's grateful face flashed in her mind. The relief her sister had shown when Bea had found Lucinda's gown had been so obvious. Could she really leave it all to this Perry? What did he know about investigating? Hadn't he been a tour guide until recently?

No! She sat up straight, dislodging Daisy's head from her knees, and grabbed her laptop. As she scrolled through her notes, a thought struck her like lightning. *Can that be it?* She grabbed her phone, her fingers stabbing the keypad. She needed to make that call she'd not got around to yet…

Perry's footsteps echoed in the empty hallway as he trudged back to his office, a garment bag slung over one shoulder.

He'd been home to shower and pick up his dinner jacket and was ready for the event, but he wasn't looking forward to it. He'd failed to identify the saboteur, and now he'd crossed off his last suspect. On his way back here, he'd stopped off at the security gate and discovered that Sally had left at lunchtime. Way before Lucinda's gown had been taken. She couldn't be the dress thief. Sarah had told him what Lady Beatrice had seen, and her description ruled out Nat and Greg. So that was that. He was back to square one, along with a nagging worry that the real culprit might have more mischief planned. *But who?*

As Perry reached his office door and turned the key in the lock, he remembered what Simon had told him just before he'd left home. "Go back over everything. Your notes. Your suspects. All of it. Something will click." Sage advice, of course, but easier said than done. Perry felt like he'd examined the facts from every angle already. Without some sort of divine inspiration, what more could he possibly do?

Hanging up his garment bag, he went to the coffee machine on the sideboard and popped a capsule in. As he waited for it to do its magic, he gave himself a pep talk. *Come on, Perry. Sarah's counting on you.* He needed to prove to her that his promotion was justified. He also had a nagging suspicion that Sarah's sister was doing some sleuthing of her own. *Well, you can't let that spoiled madam work it out before you!*

Feeling more positive, he took his coffee and settled behind his desk. He placed the steaming cup down, and his fingers together in a steeple formation. He leaned back in his chair. What did he know? He closed his eyes.

Suddenly, a memory surfaced. He was in the kitchen with Sarah. Nat was bawling at his junior chefs. Perry squeezed his eyes tighter. Something the chef had said had sounded familiar. What was it? *Ah, that's it!* He'd yelled, "If you think this is acceptable, you should raise your standards!" Perry had heard that phrase before. His eyes shot open. *The party favours!*

He grabbed the wastepaper bin, delving into the mound of white slips of paper. *Ah-ha! 'If you think you're classy, you should raise your standards.'* His heart raced as he stared at the message. It couldn't be a coincidence, could it? Then his stomach dropped. But there was no way Nat could have got away from the kitchen and taken Lucinda's dress. *So how did he do it?* His mind swirled with possibilities. *Ah!* What if Nat was in on it with someone else? *Sally!* Although she'd left around noon, what if she'd come back sometime later? He hadn't asked security if she'd returned, only when she'd left!

Excited, he grabbed his coffee mug and lifted it to his lips. *Ouch!* It was hot. He jerked the cup away from him. As he returned it to the desk, his elbow caught the edge of a stack of papers.

"Oh, for the love of—" He yelped, watching in horror as coffee splashed over his fingers and across his desk.

Frantically, he snatched at the soggy documents, his heart racing. He swept them off the table and shook them. One particular sheet caught his eye—the guest list changes he'd scribbled down after Sarah's original sheet had vanished. Coffee dripped from its edges, but as it caught the light, something made him pause.

He squinted, tilting his head. "No way... How did I miss that?"

19

FIFTEEN MINUTES BEFORE THE PARTY...

Bea raced down the stairs, her boots thudding on the marble steps. Daisy galloped ahead of her, the little dog's pink tongue hanging out.

Bea's heart pounded in time with her footsteps as she followed Daisy. *I must find Sarah before it's too late.* The pieces had finally slotted into place during that last phone call. Bea was fairly sure she knew who it was. She reached the bottom of the staircase and landed on the black-and-white floor of the Painted Hall. Servers in crisp uniforms bustled about in the entrance with trays of champagne flutes ready to be handed to arriving guests.

As Bea and Daisy crept along the side of one wall, she spotted Jasmine Curson over by the main door, beautifully dressed in a long, elegant shimmering number, ready to greet the guests. *I should've changed into something more formal.* But there hadn't been time. Not when a troublemaker was on the loose, possibly plotting their next move right under their noses.

She slipped around the corner and hurried down the hallway. Guests would be arriving any minute for the celebrations. The saboteur could strike again, this time with an audience. Bea's stomach churned at the thought. It would be a media disaster for Sarah if something happened in front of all those influential people. *I need to warn her. Fast!*

Perry's heart rate soared as he dashed through the corridor, his polished Oxfords tapping against the marble floor. It wasn't long before the first guests were due to arrive. He was cutting it fine. He tugged at his bow tie. At least he was suitably dressed. In fact, he was looking sharp, even if he said so himself. *Now if only these blasted shoes didn't feel like medieval torture devices.*

He winced as he rounded the corner, his pinched toes protesting with every step. But there was no time to dwell on discomfort. His mind whirred with the revelation he'd pieced together. His blue eyes narrowed. Simon had been right. It had all finally clicked. He needed to find Sarah and tell her before any more damage was done…

Bea pushed open the door to the Red Ballroom and entered the elaborate room, Daisy following. Crystal chandeliers glittered overhead, and in the middle of the ceiling, the new floral centrepiece sparkled with crystal teardrops. She searched the room with her eyes. No Sarah. *Where is she?*

Daisy gave a *woof* as a tall man burst into the ballroom. Sarah's assistant was dressed to the nines in a beautifully fitted dinner jacket, but he seemed to be limping.

His eyes darted around the ballroom, a frown etched on his face.

What's he doing here? Did he know too? Was he also trying to find Sarah? *I must get to her first!*

Perry scanned for Lady Sarah's elegant figure. The room sparkled with opulence, but he barely noticed, focused solely on finding his boss.

Then his eyes locked on to Lady Beatrice, and he did a double take. *What in the world is she wearing? A long black jumper, jeans, and boots!* Perry's fashion-conscious mind reeled at the sight. *Has she mistaken this for a barn dance?* he thought, his eyebrow arching involuntarily. And what was she doing here anyway? And why did she have her cute little dog with her? *This isn't a party for dogs!*

Perry straightened his suit jacket as he looked away, his eyes continuing to roam the room for Sarah. Just then, she swept in through the open doors, resplendent in a long deep-red gown. Her dark hair was piled high in an elegant bun, her makeup flawless as always.

"Sarah!" he called out and began to move. To his dismay, Lady Beatrice was converging on her sister from the other direction.

Perry's competitive streak flared.

"Oh no, you don't," he muttered, picking up his pace despite the stabbing pain in his feet. "I solved this first, and I'll be blowed if I let you steal my thunder."

"Sarah!" Bea called out, her voice more urgent than she'd intended. She could hear the *pitter-patter* of Daisy's paws combined with Perry's laboured breathing as they all converged on the startled hostess.

The guests would be arriving any minute. *I have to be quick.* As she reached Sarah, the words tumbled out. "I know—"

"—who did it!" Perry blurted. His eyes darted to Bea, his brows furrowing. What had she said? Her face mirrored his confusion. *She knows? Or does she? Maybe she only thinks she does…*

Sarah held up a hand, glancing around. "Keep your voices down," she hissed under her breath. "The guests will be here soon." She gestured towards the staff door, her expression serious. "Come with me, both of you. We need to discuss this in private."

Perry glared at Bea as she scooped up her small white terrier, then he turned and followed Sarah. As his boss drifted across the room, Perry was aware of the sound of Bea's boots close behind him, scuffing the immaculately polished floor. *Really!*

The door clicked shut behind the three of them. The corridor was empty.

"Alright," Sarah said, crossing her arms and lifting a sculpted eyebrow. "Who's our mystery insurgent?"

Bea lifted her chin as she glanced at Perry. *I'm going first!*

She turned to her sister and opened her mouth. Suddenly, a piercing sound split the air.

The fire alarm blared through the building, its urgent wail sending a chill down her spine.

"Oh no," Bea whispered, hugging a trembling Daisy to her chest as her heart sank. *It looks like it's not over yet.*

20

TEN MINUTES BEFORE THE PARTY…

The fire alarm blared, a relentless screech that set Bea's teeth on edge. Her heart raced as she sprinted down the corridor, Daisy charging ahead of her. Sarah trailed behind them, her heels and gown slowing her progress.

She couldn't believe Perry had cried out the same name as her just as the alarm had come on. At least it had strengthened her resolve. She *was* right about who the guilty party was. *But I need to find them now!*

Argh, this noise. Come on, Perry. Turn it off. Perry hadn't looked too pleased when Sarah had asked him to deal with the alarm and then reassure Jas and Lucinda that everything was alright. Bea got the feeling he would rather be in on the action.

She passed the kitchens, a cacophony of clattering pots and pans adding to the noisy chaos around her. Bea's mind whirred. The guests would arrive any minute. *This has to be resolved quickly.*

Suddenly, Daisy skidded to a halt, barking furiously at an open door ahead. *The events office!* Bea reached it as the alarm cut off, leaving an eerie silence in its wake. She darted into the room, Daisy at her heels. She halted abruptly. A figure in gloves stood with their back to her, hunched over the far side desk, shaking a squeezy bottle of red paint. *What on earth?*

Then her attention was caught by an orange BBQ lighter on the desk nearest her. She crept forward and snatched it. Her fingers closed around the warm plastic tip. *This must be what was used to set off the alarm.*

Sarah, somewhat out of breath and holding up her dress with one hand, locked eyes with Bea as she entered the room. A silent understanding passed between them. *We've got her!*

Sarah turned to the figure. "Evie," she said, her voice firm but gentle. "This needs to stop now."

The woman's head snapped around as she noticed them for the first time. A sneer twisted her lips. "Stop? Oh, no. I'm far from finished," she spat, her pale face scrunched up.

Bea's skin crawled. The usually warm hazel eyes of the party planner now had a dangerous glint in them. *Maybe we should've waited and called security before we came charging in to confront her?* Bea had underestimated how far this would escalate. *Now what are we going to do?*

"Whatever you're planning, Evie, it's not worth it," Sarah said firmly, holding up a placating hand as she took a step forward.

Suddenly, Evie grabbed the plastic bottle full of paint and clutched it to her. Bea's breath caught as she saw what had been hiding behind it: a yellow plastic bottle. *What's that?* Her eyes strained to read the label. *Bleach?* Panic rose in her chest. *That can do some serious damage.*

Sarah started moving closer to Evie, her hand outstretched. "Please, let's talk about this."

Evie snatched up the bottle of bleach, her knuckles white around its neck. She held both containers in front of her.

Bea's legs turned to jelly. *Sarah, be careful!* "Stop!" Bea cried out, her voice sharp with fear. "Don't go any closer, Sarah!"

"Very wise, my lady," Evie said, shaking the containers menacingly. "I don't want to hurt anyone. But I will if you don't back off."

Sarah's voice quivered as she took a step backwards. "Why, Evie? Why Lucinda?"

"You don't understand!" Evie cried, her voice now rising. "Lucinda deserves this. She ruined my life!"

Bea's heart clenched. "It's because she bullied you at school, isn't it?" Her cousin Sophie had told her on the phone that Lucinda had given Evie a hard time at school, and eventually, her parents had taken her away. That was what had made Bea realise Evie had a strong motive to disrupt the event. And, of course, she had access to all areas of the house.

Evie's face contorted. "Yes," she hissed. "That cow made my life hell."

Bea's mind raced. She had to defuse this situation before it escalated. "Evie, please. Let's talk about this."

"Talk?" The woman scoffed. "Like Lucinda talked to me in school? No, I don't think so."

"Whatever Lucinda did, this isn't the answer." Sarah held her chin up, but Bea noticed her hands were trembling.

"You don't know what she did," Evie spat. "But she'll learn. She'll see how it feels."

Bea's heart thumped in her chest. She needed to keep the party planner talking to buy time. "But why now, Evie? This all happened a long time ago."

Evie's face contorted with a mix of pain and rage. "When I first found out she was the client, I only wanted to ruin her party. You know, so it wasn't this perfect thing that she was demanding. But then..." She paused, her breath catching. "She showed up at Posh and Fabulous two days ago. She recognised me instantly, and she started with the threats again. This time she said she would get me fired if her party wasn't exactly as she wanted. She told me I'd never work in event planning again."

A bitter laugh escaped Evie's lips. "As if I care. This was never my first choice for a job… But seeing her... It brought everything back. All the pain, the humiliation. And I'm fed up with it! I'm an adult now, not some scared little kid. So I'm going to give her a taste of her own medicine."

Bea's stomach churned. How could she stop this with no one getting hurt? She desperately wished she knew some kind of restraining technique, anything to stop Evie before things got any worse. She looked hopefully at her sister, but Sarah seemed to have frozen on the spot. *Shall I keep her talking? Is that the right thing to do?* "Evie," she said softly. "What exactly did Lucinda do to you?"

Tears welled up in the woman's eyes. "At first, it was name calling and laughing at me because I liked science. But when I didn't react, she started to take the treats I'd received from home that I kept in my locker. I tried to ignore her, but it just seemed to spur her on even more." Her voice cracked as she continued, "So it got worse. My parents sent me a birthday cake, and Lucinda 'accidentally' dropped it. It was ruined. She spilled coffee, again 'accidentally', on the special dress my parents had had made for me for the end-of-term party. I had nothing else to wear, so I couldn't go. But the worst," she said, her voice wobbling, "was my stuffed elephant. My grandmother had given it to me just before she'd died. Lucinda stole it, then covered it in paint. She called it 'art', and everyone laughed."

Bea watched as Evie's composure crumbled, her anger

giving way to raw pain. She longed to rush forward and stop this, but fear kept her rooted in place. While Evie had that bottle of bleach in her hand, she was too dangerous to approach.

Suddenly, Evie straightened up, her face hardening into a mask of determination. She looked down at the bottles in her hand. "Well," she said. "Let's see if Lucinda thinks she's a work of art when I'm done with her dress, shall we?"

In a flash, Evie bolted for the door. Forgetting the danger, Bea lunged to intercept her, but she shoved past, sending Bea stumbling back.

"Evie, no!" Sarah yelled as she grabbed the bottom of her own dress and hurtled out of the door. Daisy followed, barking as Bea regained her footing and took off after both of them. Dread knotted her stomach. She had to catch Evie before it was too late and Lucinda's party turned into a disaster none of them could ever come back from.

21

TWO MINUTES BEFORE THE PARTY...

Bea raced down the hall, her heartbeat pounding in her ears. Evie's footsteps echoed ahead, punctuated by Sarah's clicking heels. As Bea overtook her sister, Daisy was by her side barking, excited by the game of chase.

"Stop, Evie! Please," Bea shouted, her voice now almost hoarse.

But the party planner didn't slow down as she darted around the corner, her dark bob bouncing. As Bea reached the turn, the kitchen door burst open. A server stumbled out, a tray of glasses in hand.

Crash!

Evie collided with him, sending the glasses flying. The yellow bottle of bleach slipped from her grasp and headed towards the wooden floor.

"Daisy, no!" Bea screamed, her eyes wide with panic. Daisy bounded forward, her nose twitching curiously. Icy fear shot through Bea's veins. *Daisy!*

With a clatter, the bottle hit the floor, then bounced. Bea held her breath. It landed again and rolled to a stop a few inches from Daisy's front paw. The lid remained intact. Bea clutched the side of the wall as her knees gave way. Evie scrambled to her feet, leaving the bottle of bleach behind. She took off running again. Daisy jumped over the obstacle, then charged after her, barking.

As Bea pushed herself off the wall and gave chase, guilt gnawed at her insides. *I pushed Evie too hard. This is my fault.*

They rounded the last bend. The ornate doors that opened into the Painted Hall loomed ahead. Outside of them, Lucinda would be greeting her eager guests at any moment. Bea's stomach lurched. *We're too late.*

Suddenly, the doors flew open. Adrian Breen charged in with two burly security officers. The guards lunged forward, grabbing Evie's arms. She thrashed around for a few seconds, then went limp in their grasp. The bottle of paint dropped from her loose fingers.

"Daisy!" Bea shouted breathlessly. "Can someone grab her?" Adrian lurched forward and scooped Daisy up in his arms just as the bottle hit the floor. It bounced once, then rolled away, stopping when it hit the wall. Bea slowed to a stop, then caught her breath. "Thanks, Adrian. I didn't want her getting covered in paint."

Sarah caught up, placing a hand on Bea's shoulder. "Thank goodness it's over," she murmured. Bea nodded, unable to speak.

As the two men led Evie past Bea, their eyes briefly met. The young woman's face looked almost calm, all her fight drained away. Despite everything, Bea felt a pang of sympathy for her.

The door opened, and Jas appeared with Perry behind her. "What on earth is going on?" she demanded.

Perry's heart rate slowed as he took in the scene before him. Evie, subdued and defeated, was being held by two security personnel half-way along the corridor. He let out a slow breath. *They've got her!* His decision to call security after Sarah and her sister hadn't reappeared had been the right one.

By the wall, Adrian Breen was holding Lady Beatrice's little dog in his arms and talking to her dishevelled and pink-faced owner. Just to the side of them was Sarah. She was smoothing down her dress, clearly trying to regain her composure. She took a deep breath and stepped forward. "I'll talk to you in a minute, Jas." Her voice was a little shaky but still firm. She turned to him. "Perry, I need you to go back into the Painted Hall and make sure everything is alright with Lucinda as she greets the guests. We can't let this... incident disrupt the evening."

Perry looked from Sarah to Jas and back. *But I want to know what happened!* His lips thrust forward in a pout. *I called security. I identified Evie as the culprit. Don't I deserve an explanation too?*

"Please, Perry?" Sarah said. "I know you can handle Lucinda for me."

Perry suppressed a groan. *I suppose so...* He pushed his shoulders back. "I'm on it." As he spun around, Adrian Breen's voice caught his attention. "Good girl, Daisy," the man said. "Your barking led us right to them."

Really? Perry rolled his eyes as he pushed open the door. Even the dog was getting more credit than him.

In the Painted Room, crystal chandeliers sparkled overhead, casting a warm glow on the gilded walls. Over by the lobby of the main entrance, Lucinda and her parents were poised like royalty, ready to greet the first arrivals, due any second.

He took a quick breath. *Come on, Perry!* It was up to him

to distract Lucinda from any whispers of trouble. He straightened his suit jacket, plastered on his most winning smile, and strode across the opulent room.

Lucinda's perfectly arched eyebrow rose as he approached. "What's going on?" she demanded, her voice sharp. "Where are Jasmine and Lady Sarah?"

Perry flashed his most disarming smile. "Just taking care of some last-minute details. Everything is ready."

She narrowed her eyes. "Remind me who you are again..."

How many times had they met? *You really are a piece of work!* For a second, he rather wished they hadn't stopped Evie from ruining Lucinda's party. He fought to keep the irritation from his voice. "I'm Perry. Sarah's assistant."

"Well, Perry, Sarah's assistant, they'd better hurry," the birthday girl huffed. "Our guests are arriving!"

Perry nodded, his gaze drifting to the massive doors swinging open to admit the first elegant couples. He stepped back as Lucinda greeted her friends with air kisses and effusive compliments.

Strolling outside to check on the valets, Perry breathed in the crisp evening air. The queue of luxury vehicles snaked impressively down the drive. A sleek sports car suddenly roared up, brazenly cutting the line. It screeched to a halt, and a dashing man in a tuxedo jumped out, carelessly tossing his keys to a startled valet.

"There's always one," Perry muttered to himself.

As the man sauntered towards the entrance, Perry's stomach sunk. He recognised that cocky stride, that chiselled jaw.

Danny Roe. Famous footballer and Lucinda's ex-fiancé.

And definitely not on the guest list.

As Perry hurried towards security at the bottom of the

steps leading to the house, it crossed his mind to let Danny in. It would serve Lucinda right. *But no, that wouldn't be professional.* He arrived at the same time as Danny reached the security post.

"Invitation, sir?" the guard asked, reaching out his hand.

Danny's charming smile faltered. "Don't you know who I am?"

Perry stepped in. "Mr Roe, could I have a word, please?" He led Danny aside as security hovered nearby. "I'm afraid there's been a misunderstanding. You're not on the guest list."

Danny's jaw clenched. "This is ridiculous! I'm Lucinda's—"

"Ex-fiancé," Perry finished quietly, emphasising the 'ex'. "Please, let's not make a scene. The paparazzi will have a field day."

For a moment, Perry thought Danny might argue. Then the man's shoulders slumped, and he nodded slowly. With a last glance up at the front of Francis Court, Danny Roe turned and walked back to his car.

Phew! Another crisis averted!

Perry strode back into the house, his heart rate slowing down. The Painted Hall buzzed with activity, a sea of glittering gowns and black bow ties. He scanned the room, relieved when he spotted Sarah and Jas with Lucinda's family.

He suddenly felt slightly giddy. *It's over.*

Sarah glanced up, meeting his gaze across the room. With a subtle tilt of her head, she excused herself from the group and glided towards him. "Perry," she greeted in a low voice as she drew him into a corner. "I wanted to thank you for your quick thinking earlier. Calling security was absolutely the right move."

A flush of pride at her words washed over him, then his curiosity kicked in. "Why did she do it?"

Sarah explained concisely what had happened when she and her sister had found Evie in the events office, planning her final act of revenge on Lucinda. Perry felt a chill run through him as Sarah told him about how Lucinda had treated Evie at school. Never having been one to hide his light under a bushel, Perry had been the target of a certain amount of bullying when he'd been younger. He understood those scars ran deep.

Perry frowned. "Do you think she might try something else?"

Sarah shook her head. "She's in police custody, and I'll be informing Lucinda and her family of the potential risk tomorrow before they leave. Just to be on the safe side." She placed a hand on his arm, her touch light but meaningful. "I truly appreciate all your support throughout this, Perry. Your instincts and dedication have been invaluable."

A warm glow spread through his chest. "I'm happy I could help."

"You did more than help. You were instrumental in identifying Evie as the culprit." She tipped her head to one side. "So how did you know it was her?"

Perry grinned. "If I'm being totally honest, it was an accident, really. You remember when we lost the guest list, and Evie gave me a piece of paper from her planner to write the updates on?"

Sarah nodded.

"Well, when the paper had the light behind it, I could see an imprint of Evie's writing. Something she'd been doing that had gone through to the sheet she gave me."

"What was it?" Sarah asked, her eyes wide.

"A list of insulting phrases like the ones that were in the party favours!" he replied triumphantly.

"Good spot!" Sarah said, smiling. "Well, I couldn't have done this without you."

A smile tugged at his lips. "Thank you, Sarah. That means a lot."

She squeezed his arm before releasing it. "Right, then. We'd better get back to it. We still have a birthday party to oversee."

With a grin, Perry offered her his elbow. "Let's go, my lady."

Bea curled up on the sofa in her apartment, her legs tucked underneath her, a glass of Tia Maria clasped in one hand, while her other rested on Daisy's head. She sipped her drink. The roasted coffee notes danced on her tongue, followed by a gentle warmth as it spread down her throat. *Delicious...*

She was aware of the distant hum of the party going on two floors below her. Sarah had suggested to Bea that she get changed and joined them, but the thought of celebrating the birthday of a despicable bully like Lucinda Hamilton held no appeal for her. Having stood next to Sarah and Jas and watched the newly-sacked Evie being escorted away earlier this evening, Bea had no desire to see Lucinda ever again. In fact, a part of her wished they'd not stopped Evie 'painting' Lucinda's dress. But only a small part. Her wish to see Evie's tormentor humiliated was not as strong as her need for the event to be a tremendous success for Sarah's sake.

With a sigh, Daisy sat up. After slowly spinning in a circle twice, she curled up into a tight ball and closed her eyes. Bea took another sip of her drink, then placed the small glass on the table in front of her as her phone vibrated next to it.

Sarah: *Just wanted to say how grateful I am for your help and support this week. I couldn't have done it without you, sis. Thank you xx*

Bea smiled smugly. *Indeed.* She'd done alright for someone whose only knowledge of solving murder mysteries had been gained from watching crime shows on television with her son.

She pulled her fluffy robe around her, her limbs feeling heavy as she snuggled down into the corner of the couch.

At least it hadn't been a murder!

22

THE DAY AFTER THE PARTY

The Society Page online article:

<u>Lucinda Hamilton's 30th: A Modern Fairy Tale Come to Life</u>

Francis Court was utterly transformed this weekend for Lucinda Hamilton's highly anticipated 30th birthday party, an event that has already been dubbed "the event of the year" by attendees. Hosted at the prestigious ancestral home of the Astley family and coordinated by the King's niece, Lady Sarah Rosdale, the evening attracted an exclusive guest list of influencers and high-profile figures from London's social scene.

The event, staged by the esteemed party planners Posh and Fabulous, transformed the stately venue into a modern fairy tale, complete with enchanting decor, exquisite dining, and live entertainment that kept guests dancing well into the night.

Guests were welcomed into a glittering wonderland, with towering crystal-embedded floral installations in blush pinks and soft creams and crystal chandeliers casting golden glows over tables dressed in shimmering linens and accented by gilded candelabras. One guest remarked, "Walking in felt like stepping into a dream. Every detail was absolutely exquisite."

The atmosphere was jubilant, and many guests took to Instagram to share photos under the hashtag #Lucindas-FairyTale30. "I've been to countless events, but this was something else entirely," said a well-known socialite. "It wasn't just a party—it was an experience. The organisers outdid themselves, and Francis Court has set a benchmark of excellence for event hosting."

Lucinda herself stole the spotlight in a gold couture gown that glittered as much as the event itself. "She looked like a true princess," gushed another attendee. "It was impossible to take your eyes off her." Rumours are Lucinda's ex-fiancé, footballer Danny Roe, had tried to gatecrash the event, but he was turned away at the door.

The night concluded with a dazzling fireworks display over the estate, accompanied by cheers and applause from the crowd. There seems to be no question that Francis Court has now put itself firmly on the map as a gold standard venue and can look forward to hosting many more events like this in the future.

I hope you enjoyed *A Toast to Trouble*. If you did then please consider writing a review on Amazon or Goodreads, or even both. It helps me a lot if you let people know that you recommend it.

Want to know how Perry and Bea end up best friends? Read more about life (and death) at Francis Court in *Spruced up for Murder*, the first in the *A Right Royal Cozy Investiga-*

tion series, available in the Amazon store or wherever you get your paperbacks. **You can read chapter 1 on the next page…**

For other books by me, take a look at the back pages.

If you want to find out more about what I'm up to you can find me on Facebook at *helengoldenauthor* or on Instagram at *helengolden_author*.

Be the first to know when my next book is available. Follow Helen Golden on Amazon, BookBub, and Goodreads to get alerts whenever I have a new release, preorder, or a discount on any of my books.

CHAPTER 1 PREVIEW - SPRUCED UP FOR MURDER

Early morning, Wednesday 7 April

"Oh my giddy aunt!" Perry Juke slapped his hand up to his mouth, his face turning pale as he gawped at the body in front of them.

"Oh my giddy aunt, indeed," Lady Beatrice, the Countess of Rossex, replied, gazing at the prone form lying only a few metres away from her. Her stomach twisted at the sight of his lifeless body. Instinctively, she wanted to look away, but like a moth attracted to a light, she was drawn to the scene before her.

He — for it was definitely a man with his stocky frame and shaved head — was lying on his front, his arms and legs splayed out, looking rather like he had fallen from a great height. Blood obscured the right-hand side of his face. A patch of what looked like red wine had soaked into the green and black Persian rug underneath his body. The grey marble table, which was normally by the side of the olive-green leather Chesterfield, was lying askew on the floor. One corner was covered in something dark and sticky.

"He must have fallen and hit his head on the table. Is he dead? He looks very dead," Perry said, scanning the room as if searching for someone to confirm the body was, indeed, dead.

Bea raised her hand to her chest to still her racing heart.

The press is going to love this.

A dead body at Francis Court, found by a member of the royal family — this was gold.

She raked her slim fingers through her long auburn hair. If only she hadn't been guilted by her mother into accepting her sister's request to take on the interior design of the refurbished Events Suite, she would be upstairs in her apartment right now, enjoying a leisurely coffee and snuggling with her dog, Daisy. Shaking her head, she returned to the matter in hand. There was possibly a dead body in front of them, and it had to be dealt with.

I suppose one of us needs to check for a pulse.

She turned hopefully to Perry.

Read more of *Spruced Up For Murder* by ordering your copy NOW from the Amazon store or wherever you buy your paperbacks.

CHARACTERS IN ORDER OF APPEARANCE

A TOAST TO TROUBLE

Lady Beatrice — The Countess of Rossex. Seventeenth in line to the British throne. Daughter of Charles Astley, the Duke of Arnwall and Her Royal Highness Princess Helen. Niece of the current king.

Lady Sarah Rosdale — Lady Beatrice's elder sister. Manages events at Francis Court.

Lucinda Hamilton — model and heiress whose 30th birthday party is taking place at Francis Court.

Nathan 'Nat' Harper — head chef for Posh and Fabulous.

Evie Hayes — party planner at Posh and Fabulous.

Jasmin Curson — co-manager at Posh and Fabulous party planners.

Sir Leo Hamilton — owner of the Scottish based shipping line SCH. Lucinda's father.

Dame Katherine Hamilton — opera singer. Mother of Lucinda. Friend of HRH Princess Helen.

Danny Roe — Footballer. Lucinda's ex-fiancé.

Charles Astley — Duke of Arnwall. Lady Beatrice's father.

HRH Princess Helen — Duchess of Arnwall. Mother of Lady Beatrice. Sister of the current king.

King James — King of England. Princess Helen's brother and Lady Beatrice's uncle.

Sam Wiltshire — son of Lady Beatrice and the late James Wiltshire, the Earl of Rossex. Future Earl of Durrland.

James Wiltshire — The Earl of Rossex. Lady Beatrice's late husband killed in a car accident eleven years ago.

Perry Juke — Lady Sarah's executive assistant.

Robert (Robbie) Rosdale — Lady Sarah's son.

Charlotte (Lottie) Rosdale — Lady Sarah's daughter.

John Rosdale — Lady Sarah's husband.

Simon Lattimore — Perry Juke's partner. Bestselling crime writer. Ex-Fenshire CID.

Daisy — Lady Beatrice's adorable West Highland Terrier.

Lady Sophie Clifford — Bea's cousin on her mother's side.

Greg Morton — Maintenance man at Francis Court.

Sally Wells — cleaner who works for a cleaning company employed by Posh and Fabulous.

Mrs Crammond — head housekeeper at Francis Court.

Claire Beck — friend of Perry Juke. Works in Human Resources at Francis Court.

Adrian Breen — head of security at Francis Court. Ex-Fenshire CID.

Ward — the Astley family's driver and overseer of maintenance at Francis Court.

Holly Curson — co-manager at Posh and Fabulous.

Earl and Countess of Durrland — the late James Wiltshire's parents and Sam's grandparents.

ALSO BY HELEN GOLDEN

A short prequal in the series A Right Royal Cozy Investigation. Can Perry Juke and Simon Lattimore work together to solve the mystery of the missing clock before the thief disappears? FREE novelette when you sign up to my readers' club. See end of final chapter for details. Ebook only.

First book in the A Right Royal Cozy Investigation series. Amateur sleuth, Lady Beatrice, must pit her wits against Detective Chief Inspector Richard Fitzwilliam to prove her sister innocent of murder. With the help of her clever dog, her flamboyant co-interior designer and his ex-police partner, can she find the killer before him, or will she make a fool of herself?

Second book in the A Right Royal Cozy Investigation series. Amateur sleuth, Lady Beatrice, must once again go up against DCI Fitzwilliam to find a killer. With the help of Daisy, her clever companion, and her two best friends, Perry and Simon, can she catch the culprit before her childhood friend's wedding is ruined?

The third book in the A Right Royal Cozy Investigation series. When DCI Richard Fitzwilliam gets it into his head that Lady Beatrice's new beau Seb is guilty of murder, can the amateur sleuth, along with the help of Daisy, her clever westie, and her best friends Perry and Simon, find the real killer before Fitzwilliam goes ahead and arrests Seb?

A Prequel in the A Right Royal Cozy Investigation series. When Lady Beatrice's husband James Wiltshire dies in a car crash along with the wife of a member of staff, there are questions to be answered. Why haven't the occupants of two cars seen in the accident area come forward? And what is the secret James had been keeping from her?

When the dead body of the event's planner is found at the staff ball that Lady Beatrice is hosting at Francis Court, the amateur sleuth, with help from her clever dog Daisy and best friend Perry, must catch the killer before the partygoers find out and New Year's Eve is ruined.

Snow descends on Drew Castle in Scotland cutting the castle off and forcing Lady Beatrice along with Daisy her clever dog, and her best friends Perry and Simon to cooperate with boorish DCI Fitzwilliam to catch a killer before they strike again.

A murder at Gollingham Palace sparks a hunt to find the killer. For once, Lady Beatrice is happy to let DCI Richard Fitzwilliam get on with it. But when information comes to light that indicates it could be linked to her husband's car accident fifteen years ago, she is compelled to get involved. Will she finally find out the truth behind James's tragic death?

An unforgettable bachelor weekend for Perry filled with luxury, laughter, and an unexpected death.
Can Bea, Perry, and his hen's catch the killer before the weekend is over?

Bake Off Wars is being filmed on site at Francis Court and everyone is buzzing. But when much-loved pastry chef and judge, Vera Bolt, is found dead on set, can Bea, with the help of her best friend Perry, his husband Simon, and her cute little terrier, Daisy, expose the killer before the show is over?

Even in a charming seaside town, secrets don't stay buried for long as Bea and Perry discover when they uncover the remains of a chef who disappeared 3 years ago. As they unravel a web of professional rivalries and buried grudges, they must race against time to solve the murder before the grand opening of Simon's new restaurant.

Lady Beatrice's peaceful holiday in Portugal is shattered when a Hollywood star's husband is found dead. What appears to be an accident soon reveals itself as murder. Tasked with clearing an innocent woman's name, Bea and Rich must untangle a web of lies to uncover the truth before it's too late.

PAPERBACKS AVAILABLE FROM WHEREVER YOU BUY YOUR BOOKS.